Books by Janet Lambert

PENNY PARRISH STORIES
Star Spangled Summer 1941
Dreams of Glory 1942
Glory Be! 1943
Up Goes the Curtain 1946
Practically Perfect 1947
The Reluctant Heart 1950

TIPPY PARRISH STORIES
Miss Tippy 1948
Little Miss Atlas 1949
Miss America 1951
Don't Cry Little Girl 1952
Rainbow After Rain 1953
Welcome Home, Mrs. Jordan 1953
Song in Their Hearts 1956
Here's Marny 1969

JORDAN STORIES
Just Jenifer 1945
Friday's Child 1947
Confusion by Cupid 1950
A Dream for Susan 1954
Love Taps Gently 1955
Myself & I 1957
The Stars Hang High 1960
Wedding Bells 1961
A Bright Tomorrow 1965

PARRI MACDONALD STORIES
Introducing Parri 1962
That's My Girl 1964
Stagestruck Parri 1966
My Davy 1968

CANDY KANE STORIES
Candy Kane 1943
Whoa, Matilda 1944
One for the Money 1946

DRIA MEREDITH STORIES
Star Dream 1951
Summer for Seven 1952
High Hurdles 1955

CAMPBELL STORIES
The Precious Days 1957
For Each Other 1959
Forever and Ever 1961
Five's a Crowd 1963
First of All 1966
The Odd Ones 1969

SUGAR BRADLEY STORIES
Sweet as Sugar 1967
Hi, Neighbor 1968

CHRISTIE DRAYTON STORIES
Where the Heart Is 1948
Treasure Trouble 1949

PATTY AND GINGER STORIES
We're Going Steady 1958
Boy Wanted 1959
Spring Fever 1960
Summer Madness 1962
Extra Special 1963
On Her Own 1964

CINDA HOLLISTER STORIES
Cinda 1954
Fly Away Cinda 1956
Big Deal 1958
Triple Trouble 1965
Love to Spare 1967

Here's Marny

Dear Readers:

Mother always said she wanted her books to be good enough to be found in someone's attic!

After all of these years, I find her stories—not in attics at all—but prominent in fans' bookcases just as mine are. It is so heart-warming to know that through these republications she will go on telling good stories and being there for her "girls," some of whom find no other place to turn.

With a heart full of love and pride–
Janet Lambert's daughter,
Jeanne Ann Vanderhoef

Here's Marny

by Janet Lambert

Image Cascade Publishing

www.imagecascade.com

A hardcover edition of this book was originally published by E. P. Dutton & Co. It is here reprinted by arrangement with Mrs. Jeanne Ann Vanderhoef.

First *Image Cascade Publishing* edition published 2000.

Library of Congress Cataloging in Publication Data
Lambert, Janet 1895-1973
    Here's Marny.

(Juvenile Girls)
Reprint. Originally published: New York: E. P. Dutton, 1969.

ISBN 978-1-930009-25-7

FOR LOU ALLIE

Here's Marny

1

Marny stood before her cheap pine dresser, solemnly surveying her reflection in the splotchy mirror that hung above it. She saw a small, wistful face that seemed to be all big gray eyes under a straight slash of brown bang. She wasn't looking for beauty because she was sure she had none. The nearest thing to a compliment that she could remember ever having received in all her fifteen years was when the matron in the Children's Welfare Home, after leading her in to meet prospective parents, had praised her enthusiastically, "Marny Alexander is such a dear child"; or when Mrs. Bullock, her current foster mother, would say, "You look very nice, Marny." She was wondering what to do about her hair because she would be going clear across the city of Atlanta to baby-sit for Major and Mrs. Jordon.

It was such unsatisfactory hair, Marny thought, wishing she could afford to buy an end-curl home permanent. She couldn't, so she reached into the top drawer of the dresser and took out a candy box that held her small supply of neatly rolled ribbons. The hair that disappointed her was a thick, glossy brown with the patina of a polished chestnut, and it hugged her slender stem of neck, refusing to curl up or cup under, even though she brushed and brushed it and put its ends over rollers at night.

The white ribbon will have to do, she thought regretfully. I should have blue, but the blue one is too frayed. It was so important to look exactly right for the Jordons. Mrs. Jordon was so sweet, and so were little Tippy Two and Petey. Major Jordon? She was always shy with Major Jordon because he was an army officer, but she admired him from a distance. Eager to see them all again, she bent her head to slip the ribbon under her hair, then tied it in a precise bow with the ends the exact length of the loops.

"Marny?" Mrs. Bullock called from below. "It's time for you to go."

"I'm almost ready."

Marny gave her hair one last brushing, straightened the straps on her slip, and reached behind her for the blue-and-white-checked dress that hung on the open door of an old-fashioned wardrobe. She didn't have to move to take the dress from its hanger because the room was so narrow. She stepped into the cotton shift, careful not to wrinkle it, and pulled up the concealed front zipper. She was ready. Her flat white slippers had been polished; her old white purse had been scrubbed and polished, too, and she looked as presentable as she could make herself.

"Isn't that the dress you made in sewing class?" Mrs. Bullock asked, as Marny ran lightly down the steep stairway to the living room. And when Marny nodded that it was, she went on, "It's very nicely done. Perhaps we can borrow a sewing machine from a friend of mine and you can make yourself another one this summer. Goodness knows, you need it, child."

Mrs. Bullock had grown fond of Marny. The State of Georgia paid for her care, but Mrs. Bullock had accepted her reluctantly, having made it clear to Miss Wilcox, the caseworker, that she took in only very young babies, the ones who stayed for a few weeks, a few months, or at the longest a year. But Marny, only eleven when she came, had stayed on and on, and she had turned out to be quite helpful. She tended the babies after school and at night.

Many of the babies had been adopted before they were brought to the Bullocks' and would stay only during a waiting period, until they were determined healthy and ready to be turned over to their new parents. Some found homes later and some remained until a mother could support them. Babies left, others came, and Mrs. Bullock never felt their loss. She had hoped it would be so with Marny. But it hadn't worked out that way. No adoptive parents had wanted a plain, stringy little thing like Marny, who was half grown and getting older every year.

"You'll miss your bus," Mrs. Bullock said. And she asked, "What time will you be home?"

"I don't know, but it won't be late," Marny answered, already on her way to the door. "Major and Mrs. Jordon don't think I should be alone in the house with just the children after dark, and Major Jordon will drive me home;

he always does. Good-by." Then she jerked open the door and ran across a narrow porch and down uneven brick steps.

Mrs. Bullock watched her go, her pretty brown hair flying back, her slim legs skimming the ground; then she called her husband in from the kitchen. "George, can't you drive Marny out to the Jordons'?" she asked, as he came into the small cluttered living room, his undershirt bulging over a pair of faded tan slacks. "It's a long ride and she has to change buses in the center of town."

"Oh, she'll get there," he replied, shrugging. "She's young." George Bullock dropped his bulk into an easy chair like a bulldozer hitting bottom in an excavation. "Stop stewing about the kid," he said, scattering parts of the morning newspaper on the floor while he searched for the sports section.

"But it's so hot and she has such a long way to walk after she gets off of the bus. If you. . . ." Mrs. Bullock stopped and shook her head. "It's too late now," she said. "Here comes her bus."

Marny hopped aboard the bus, dropped her token in the coin box, and found a seat beside an open window. To air-condition the bus against the August heat would have been useless because it stopped at every second corner and great gusts of hot air poured in with the entering or alighting passengers. The heat didn't bother Marny. She was starting off to a happy day. And while some girls her age might have thought it sheer drudgery to spend a whole day with two children, a little girl of eight and a boy of five, Marny looked forward to it. It was lovely out where the Jordons lived: green lawns, green trees, and flowers.

If one wanted to sit outdoors, there was always a little breeze, and no outside heat was allowed to penetrate the plastered walls of the house. Marny loved the house because of the air conditioning. She didn't care how long the Jordons stayed away in the afternoon. She could sit in that big cool living room.

She enjoyed the children, too, Tippy Two and Petey. It was fun to play games with them, games she had never played as a child: to sit under a peach tree with crayons and scissors, to hop into a wading pool and come out dripping and cool, to chase foraging flies away from the sandwiches and malted milks she had made, then to come inside, still pretending to be an older daughter who lived there.

Of course, I couldn't be an older daughter, she thought, while she checked her purse to make sure she had the paper doll for Tippy Two and the balloons with silly faces she had bought for Petey. I'm too old to be the daughter of Major and Mrs. Jordon.

"Peach Tree Street, Peach Tree," the bus driver sang out, and she snapped shut her purse to hop off into the sweltering midtown heat.

Another bus, another long windblown ride, and Marny reached the end of her journey to a suburban area. She still had a half-mile to walk, so without bothering to comb down her bangs that had blown straight up from her forehead, she started off.

"Yoo-hoo," she heard a voice call; and looking across the street, she saw an elderly but well-kept sedan parked in the shade. "Yoo-hoo, over here," the voice called again, and she ran gratefully toward it.

"It's just plain too hot for you to walk, sugar," Tippy

Jordon said, leaning over to unlatch the door. "Hop in. I think I'm melting." And she added loudly, "Quiet in the back seat. Let Marny sit down and catch her breath."

"Did you bring us something?" Tippy Two asked eagerly, hanging over Marny and breathing hotly on her neck while Petey bounced about and demanded, "Show us what you brought."

"All right." Marny opened her purse, but their mother reached out to clap it shut again.

"When we get home," she said firmly, "you may see what Marny has for you. But right now . . ." The car left the curb with a lurch, and, quite suddenly, both children sat down. ". . . stay there," she finished, laughing as she started them off on a winding road that had fewer and fewer houses behind its tree-shaded edges. "I got a reprieve today," she told Marny as they rolled along. "Peter had a meeting with an officer who came in a few days ago, so we don't have to go to the big fund-raising smash the Women's Club is putting on. We've bought our tickets and I can stay happily at home."

"Oh, Mrs. Jordon, then you don't need me!" Marny cried, looking as if she might hop out of the car and go back the way she had come.

"Oh, but we do," Tippy Jordon assured her promptly. "We're invited to a cookout this evening, and if Peter gets home by three o'clock we have an errand we have to do. The cookout is just next door," she explained, as Marny leaned back again, "so you can look out a window and see us in the Johnstons' back yard. If you need us for anything, all you'll have to do is call and we can be home in a jiff."

"Oh, I won't need you," Marny said confidently, turning to smile at the two on the back seat who grinned winsomely back at her. "Nothing's going to go wrong, and Tippy Two and Petey always mind everything I say."

"Goodness knows why." Tippy laughed, and Marny wished she could be as pretty as Mrs. Jordon.

Her eyes were such a lovely soft amber. Her light feathery curls, even when windblown, were entrancing. She had the cutest little dimple that winked in and out at the corner of her mouth, and whenever she set her lips to speak sternly, the dimple only bored in deeper and spoiled the effect of her words.

The whole Jordon family looked like a magazine picture, Marny thought, her heart filled with love for them. They were all blond but Tippy Two, who, so Mrs. Jordon had once said, resembled her grandmother and her Aunt Penny. Petey and Major Jordon had hair so light that it looked sun-bleached, and fine gray eyes. And although Major Jordon was a slim six feet in height and Petey was a sturdy, almost chunky little boy, they walked alike and always stood with their hands resting loosely on their hips.

Marny stole another glance at the little girl who now sat so primly on the back seat. Tippy Two's eyes were an amazing violet, with long, upcurling brown lashes. Her hair was a rich, dark brown that hung straight down to end in an even line on her shoulders. She reminded Marny of the little models who pose for children's clothes in the fashion ads. Yes, they were an ideal family, Marny thought once more as the car turned into a driveway and stopped before a modest white two-storied house.

Major Jordon, in a light summer suit, was standing in the doorway of the attached garage, hands on hips as usual, and he came out to ask, "Did Old Betsy run okay today?" Then he said, "Hello, Marny."

"Hello, Major Jordon."

Marny smiled at him and listened to Mrs. Jordon exclaim:

"No. She still isn't healthy. She jumped every time I gave her gas, just as if I'd stuck a pin in her. But she did hustle along."

"I'll stop at Slim's on my way into town and have her carburetor adjusted again. Good-by, family." And as he took his place behind the wheel, he reminded, "Don't forget, Tip, that I'm to pick you up at three o'clock."

Marny went inside with Tippy Two and Petey clinging to her, while Mrs. Jordon followed with a bag of groceries. "Oh, the welcome coolness," Tippy Jordon said, putting her groceries on the kitchen counter. "Let's all sit down and enjoy it."

But hot little hands were pulling Marny through the dining room and into the living room beyond. "We can't stay now," Tippy Two sang back. "We want to see what Marny brought us."

They flopped down on the carpet; and Marny, carefully smoothing her dress under her, sat down to face them and open her purse. She produced a cellophane package with three flat, deflated balloons in it and a large envelope holding the paper doll that she had painstakingly cut out of a magazine the evening before and backed with cardboard.

"I brought some crepe paper so we can make dresses for her," she said, taking out a neat packet while Tippy Two admired the paper doll with its vacuous, smiling face. "And here are some tiny stars I found in the dime store for trimming and a paper doily that we can cut up to make lace. We can blow up the balloons first and have a sort of badminton game outdoors, and then, when we get hot and tired, we can sit in the swing under the peach tree and make dresses. We'll have fun."

Both children were cool now and ready to go outside, so each took a balloon and began to blow into it. Marny, who could have sat where she was indefinitely, picked up the third balloon and huffed and puffed. She was being paid to provide a day of watchful entertainment, so she blew until the three red, yellow, and green balls were round, then twisted the neck of each and folded it back so no air could escape.

"What are you three doing out in the heat?" she heard Mrs. Jordon call when they were running about on the grass, trying to keep the balloons in the air.

"We're playing a game," Petey shouted, whacking a balloon and sending it sailing high in the air. "Marny has a prize for the winner. Tippy Two, you missed that one."

"I know it." Tippy Two picked up the balloon and shot it back at such an angle that it hit a thorn on a rosebush and collapsed with a pop.

"Does that count against me or her?" Petey asked Marny, who was the referee and scorekeeper.

"Neither one of you," she answered, laughing. "It was an accident beyond our control." And she put the third balloon into action.

The prize was a small plastic horse; and because all the balloons met with disaster, she produced a second horse and declared the game to be a tie. "It's time to dress the paper doll now," she said, leading the way to an old canvas-cushioned glider that the Jordons had bought in a second-hand shop.

Petey had no interest in paper dolls, but at five he did like scissors and bright paper. So they sat in a row with

Marny in the middle, and when he licked a star and stuck it on crooked, she quietly pried it off and placed it where it belonged.

"It's lunchtime," Tippy Jordon called again, opening a kitchen window, then hastily closing it. And she stood watching Marny gather up the remnants of paper and crumple up all the scraps, making sure that everything was orderly before she started inside.

She was so helpful. She put potato salad and sandwiches on the children's plates. She brought them their glasses of milk from the refrigerator, saw that they tucked their paper napkins under their chins, and shoved their chairs closer to the table. She was the busiest one in the small breakfast ell that jutted off from the kitchen. She was up and down, waiting on them all, and she fed crusts of bread to the elderly French poodle that woke up from a nap and padded over to beg for food.

"Switzy wishes that you'd come every day," Tippy Jordon said, leaning down with a sliver of ham for the little dog that lifted adoring brown eyes to her. "He still gets awfully lonesome without his pal Rollo, so all he thinks about is eating."

"Rollo was our other dog," Tippy Two informed Marny. "Switzy is fifteen years old, and Mums had him before she married Daddy. Rollo must have been a hundred, because Daddy's family had him long before Daddy got in the army. He just went to sleep one night a couple of years ago and didn't wake up. He was very old."

"Almost eighteen," Tippy said, remembering the dear, frowzy little mop that Peter had adopted when he was only a boy. "We took both Switzy and Rollo to Panama with us when we were first stationed there as bride and groom.

Rollo. . . ." She stopped because Switzy lifted his head as if listening to what she was saying. He was quite deaf, she knew, but she bent down to cup his tasseled ears in her hands, and to say soothingly, "We all miss Rollo, Switzy, dear. Here's one last bite—it's all I have left, so go back to sleep."

Switzy took the meat she held out to him, swallowed it in a gulp, and padded back to his pad in the corner.

"It's nice to have pets and love them the way you do," Marny said in a constrained voice that felt tight in her throat. "I've never had any."

"You haven't?" Tippy watched her get up to take the empty plates to the sink, rinse them and put them in the dishwasher.

"I don't think I have," Marny said, coming back for the glasses. "Grandma told me that Daddy had a beagle, but I don't remember it. He used to take it hunting with him, she told me."

Tippy sat and watched her. Marny was such a dear girl. She could be pretty if someone would take a little time to show her how to be. Her hair needed shaping because her face was so small. Her dress should be shorter—not mini length, but to her knees, at least. "Look, Marny," she found herself saying, "I'll clean up the kitchen, and if you'll put the two annoying darlings down for their rest period you and I can relax in the living room."

"That sounds wonderful. I'd like to do that, so come on, kids."

Marny shooed Tippy Two and Petey before her, and they went docilely, without the usual pleas and arguments. It made their mother wonder what could accomplish such a feat. Usually this was a time of procrastination while Tippy

21

Two hunted for a special book she wanted to take with her and Petey demanded to have his radio turned on to his favorite station. She heard Marny say, "When you get up we. . . ." Then the words were lost in the upstairs hallway.

Tippy was stretched out on a long sofa that jutted out at right angles from an empty fireplace when Marny came down to join her. How do you start a conversation with a fifteen-year-old? Tippy wondered, watching Marny sit down across from her in Peter's big chair, placing her feet neatly side by side as she would in a classroom. What do you talk about? How had grownups talked to her when she was Marny's age? She didn't know. So she laid the magazine she had been reading on her chest and said, "It certainly is pleasant having you here, Marny. You haven't been here for over a month, have you?"

"No." Marny shook her neat head and answered, "You asked me to come twice and I was awfully sorry I couldn't. We had two babies then and I couldn't get away."

"Do you always take care of the babies when Mrs. Bullock has them?" Tippy asked, seizing the opening.

"Some of the time," Marny answered, "after school. When I come home I help, and on Saturdays and Sundays. When we have a tiny one that needs its night feeding I give it its two-o'clock bottle."

"Don't you have dates?" Tippy asked.

"Dates?" Marny smiled. Her mouth was pretty when she smiled. Her lips were too often pressed thinly together while her face was in repose, but when they were parted they showed their true fullness. "I don't have dates," Marny said, tight-lipped again. "There aren't any kids for me to know in the neighborhood where we live and I always come home on the school bus, so. . . ." She shrugged and explained, "I never have had children to play with so I don't mind being alone."

Tippy sat up and laid her magazine on the table beside her. "Marny," she said eagerly, "would you tell me about your life? I know you've lived with the Bullocks for four years, but what was your life like before you went there?"

"Well, you see—there was The Home," Marny said. "We always called it The Home. It's run by the Children's Welfare, and I came to the Bullocks from there."

"But what about before that? Were you born in Atlanta?" Tippy persisted, looking so interested that Marny was caught by surprise. No one had ever cared about the place of her birth before, except as a statistic to be entered in her file.

"No, I was born in Columbus, Georgia," she said; and she found herself adding, "I lived there until I was eight." She stopped then, as if she had no more facts to give; and Tippy, afraid she might not learn the true story of a child's unfortunate life, urged quickly:

"Come over here and sit beside me, Marny, and tell me all about yourself. I want very much to know."

"There isn't much to tell that's interesting," Marny said. But she got up obediently to cross the small space between them and sit down on the sofa, her slippers finding each other again and her straight little back scarcely touching the cushion behind it.

"I guess you'd like to know that I had real parents when I was little," she said. "People always like to know that, when they engage a girl for baby-sitting. They like to be sure she's legitimate and hasn't a record."

"Oh, Marny, I don't give a whoop about that!" Tippy

cried, turning sideways and laying her hand over Marny's that were clasped in her lap. "I'm only interested in you, dear."

"You are?"

Marny's big gray eyes were wide with wonder, and she listened to Tippy Jordon say, "Of course, I am. Every time you've come here I've been going out somewhere and we've never had a chance to talk. I like to know about my friends. You are my friend," she said, impulsively. "A much younger friend, but a friend. Tell me," she went on before Marny could retreat into a thoughtful digest of this news, "what were your parents like?"

"I don't remember too much about them. Mother was awfully pretty. We have some pictures of her, and Grandma said she was. Daddy. . . ." She stopped, and her gray eyes looked into Tippy's hazel ones as she said, "Thank you for calling me a friend. It makes me feel proud."

"It makes me proud, too, sugar," Tippy answered, trying to keep her voice light because she was probing into a time that might be painful to Marny. "You were going to say something about your father, weren't you?"

"Oh, yes. Daddy was big. At least I think he was," Marny said. "He looked awfully big to me when he tossed me up in the air and put me on his shoulders. He always called me Princess, I remember that. And Mother was always saying that I was her little love. We had a pretty house," Marny went on, lost now in her memories. "It had lots of grass and trees around it, and I had a rope swing with a wooden seat in it. I don't remember too much about how the house looked inside because you can't picture things exactly when you're only three. We used to go on picnics—Grandma told me we did—and I remember that I had a special little chair that Mother always put on the seat of the car so I could look out the window. I remember that all by myself, and some other things: like Daddy coming home late at night and all of us having dinner together. It wasn't night, Grandma said. It was just the early dark of wintertime. And we had an electric stove in the kitchen that I was told never to touch. And once, Mama brought home a kitten. Those are the sort of things I remember, Mrs. Jordon. Just little things, nothing big and important."

"And what happened, dear, to end that lovely time?" Tippy prodded, wishing they could continue with the memories that made Marny look dreamily into the past.

"Mother and Daddy were killed." Marny sighed and sat up even straighter. "I'll have to tell you this part the way Grandma told it to me," she said, "because I don't remember that day at all. It was just a day like any other day, I guess. Some friends of theirs had a boat, a cruiser that slept six people, and we used to go out on it to spend a whole weekend. Then one time Mother asked Grandma to come stay with me because a couple of grown-up friends were going with them. They never came back. Grandma said a storm came up and the boat broke apart when they were 'way out in the ocean."

"Oh, Marny, dear!"

"I don't remember it," Marny said, as if she were the one to comfort Tippy. "I don't remember the funeral or anything. Grandma said she bought me some new crayons and a coloring book, and a neighbor came to take care of me that day. Grandma lived in a tiny apartment then, and our house was too big for her, so she sold it and bought us a little house. It was a nice little house," Marny said reminiscently. "I was four by then, so I can remember more about it. And, of course, I lived with Grandma until I was eight."

"Did you have friends, Marny?"

"Oh, yes. When I was old enough, I went to school and I had lots of little friends. Grandma and I had good times, too. We talked about Mother and Daddy a lot because she didn't want me to ever, ever forget them."

"And then what happened that you couldn't stay with your grandmother?" Tippy asked, knowing there had to be another tragedy in Marny's life.

"Grandma fell and broke her hip," Marny related simply. "They took her to a hospital, and Aunt Birdie—she's Grandma's other daughter—came to help out. There wasn't anyone to look after me, you see, so she stayed a while. But Grandma didn't get better. Something was wrong with the bone that it wouldn't knit, the doctor said, so Aunt Birdie put Grandma in a nursing home and sold our house and brought me to Atlanta with her."

"Is your grandmother still living?" Tippy asked.

"No. Aunt Birdie said she died in the nursing home. I never did get to see her again."

"Did you have money? From the sale of the house or any insurance your father might have left you?"

Marny shook her head. "Aunt Birdie said I didn't," she replied. "She said it cost a lot to keep Grandma in the nursing home because it was quite a nice one, and that feeding and clothing me was expensive. She was always telling me that I had run out of money."

"Was she kind to you, Marny?"

"Yes, she was—at first. Then when she and Uncle Arthur began fighting so much, she wasn't. They really

26

fought, Mrs. Jordon. They didn't just quarrel; they threw things and hit each other. It scared me, so I was glad when Uncle Arthur packed up his clothes and went away one day. But after that, Aunt Birdie changed. They had rented a big apartment when I came to live with them and bought all new furniture, but after Uncle Arthur left, Aunt Birdie didn't stay home much. She made lots of new friends and sometimes she'd go away for a whole weekend, leaving just the janitor's wife to come up now and then and see if I was all right."

"*And you were how old?*" Tippy asked incredulously.

"I was ten. I got along pretty well because I knew how to cook some things, like bacon and eggs, and Aunt Birdie usually had some leftovers. But one day . . ." Marny stopped as she relived a frightening experience in her story, then went bravely on ". . . Aunt Birdie told me she couldn't afford to live there any longer. She said she had sold all the furniture and we were going to move. She didn't say where. She had packed my clothes in a big suitcase and put hers in more suitcases, and she came to school to get me. The car was full of suitcases and boxes. We drove downtown, and all she would say was, 'This isn't my fault, Marny. I've done the best I can.' She said it over and over. Then we stopped in front of a police station and she took my suitcase out of the car and told me to get out, too." Marny recited this part of her story as if she had told it many times, and Tippy was sure she had. "Aunt Birdie handed me a letter," she said, "and told me to go inside and give it to a policeman, and to take my suitcase with me."

"Oh, Marny, dear. . . ." Tippy saw not the Marny who was sitting beside her, telling her story as simply as she could, but the abandoned child standing alone on a city sidewalk. "Oh, Marny, what did you do?" she asked, tears in her eyes.

"Just what Aunt Birdie told me to," Marny answered. "I met a nice policeman just inside the door. He read the letter; then he picked up my suitcase and we went into a big room that had several more policemen in it. They were awfully good to me in there," Marny went on matter-of-factly. "One of them brought me a bottle of ginger ale and a doughnut; and they asked me a lot of questions and did a lot of telephoning before two of them left. I know now that they went to see if they could find Aunt Birdie. Of course, they couldn't. The apartment was empty. Aunt Birdie had sold the car, and it took the Bureau of Missing Persons three years to trace her to California. And then she proved that she wasn't my legal guardian and had no money to take care of me. She wrote me a letter last year and told me that she's married again and invited me to visit her sometime, but of course I never will."

"Were you frightened in the police station?" Tippy asked, her tears spilling over onto her cheeks.

"Yes, after the two policemen came back without Aunt Birdie I was. I didn't know what they would do with me, you see."

"What did they do, dear?"

"Well. . . ." Marny was silent as she considered the quickest way to end Mrs. Jordon's sympathy. Then, skipping over her two hours of silent panic, she said, "A policewoman came for me, and she took me to a place they call the Detention House. It wasn't too bad there. The people were kind to me, and there was a little girl about my age who was waiting for her mother to get out of jail. I only

28

had to stay a day longer than she did, while they were making out records and things; then they took me outside of Atlanta to the place we call The Home. Do you know about it?" she turned her head to ask.

"Not very much," Tippy said reluctantly, wishing she had served on a committee that was raising funds to buy new equipment for its playground. "They have children there who are waiting to be placed in foster homes or adopted, don't they?"

"Yes." Marny nodded, and went on, "We all hoped we'd be adopted. The babies were, and lots of the little ones while I was there, but nobody wants the older children, so they had to find foster homes for us."

"Were you unhappy in The Home, Marny?"

"No." Marny turned her big gray eyes to Tippy again and saw the tears on her cheeks. "Please don't cry, Mrs. Jordon," she pleaded. "It was better there than living with Aunt Birdie after Uncle Arthur left, or even before. The matron was darling to us, and so were the older girls who waited on the tables and saw that we got to bed at night—and Miss Wilcox. I just love Miss Wilcox." Marny's face brightened as she said, "She's the one who comes to check on me at the Bullocks', and she tried to take me home with her and keep me, but they wouldn't let her. She isn't married, you see. So she coaxed the Bullocks into taking me, even though Mrs. Bullock is registered just to take babies. She doesn't like to get fond of children, then have to worry about them when they leave. I understand how she feels."

Sounds of activity came from above them. Petey's feet hit the floor as they always did when he bounced out of bed, and Tippy Two could be heard singing in the bathroom. So Tippy, knowing this time of revelation was to be cut short, asked quickly, "Are the Bullocks good to you?"

"Oh, yes. Mrs. Bullock is really nice, and although Mr. Bullock is sort of gruff and messy, he isn't home much. He travels for a shoe firm. Oh, you musn't worry, Mrs. Jordon!" Marny cried, jumping up, ready to run upstairs to her charges. "I wish I hadn't told you all this and made you cry. I don't know why I did. You and Miss Wilcox are the only people I've ever really talked to about it."

"You talked to me because I care," Tippy answered, standing up and putting her arms around Marny. "I do care, sugar, so tell me one more thing. What will happen to you," she asked leaning back, "after you finish high school?"

"I don't know yet," Marny answered. "I'm taking typing and shorthand at school, and two night courses the high school gives, and I'm making payments on a secondhand typewriter so I can practice at home. If I can get a good job as a stenographer, I'll be able to afford to rent a room in someone's house that is approved by Miss Wilcox. If not, I'll be allowed to live in The Home until I'm eighteen. I don't know yet, but please don't worry. I'm doing fine now."

"I know you are, and you will." Tippy gave Marny a gentle pat, but she followed her to the stairway that went up from the living room, rested her arms on the newel post, and hid her face in them.

She heard Peter sounding his horn in the driveway, but she couldn't straighten up. Her compassionate tears refused to stop flowing.

2

Peter tapped the horn again, and waited. Neither the front door nor the one to the garage opened, so he got out and walked across the lawn. He expected to see Tippy come flying out, calling last-minute instructions over her shoulder, but he had almost reached the steps when she opened the front door and closed it quietly behind her. She even stopped on the small stoop to examine her face in her compact mirror.

"I thought you were in such an all-fired hurry to have me home by three o'clock," he teased good-naturedly. "You're the one who usually can't wait to get started for wherever we're going." Then he saw how solemn she looked.

"What's the matter, Childie?" he asked, using his pet name for her. "Did something go wrong with the kids?"

"No, it isn't anything I can talk about here," Tippy answered, dropping the compact back into her purse and going down to him. "We should be at the Pattersons' right now. They're expecting us, and so much depends on what we decide to tell them."

"Tippy . . ." he stopped, and turned her to face him ". . . were you crying because I have to go to Vietnam?" he asked. "You know I have to go, and we have to sell our house and get you settled somewhere else."

"It wasn't that," Tippy answered. "I'm resigned to that." Then she lifted her eyes to ask, "How did you know I'd been crying?"

"It shows." He gently closed her eyelids, then kissed each one. "Oh, Childie," he whispered wretchedly, "if only I didn't have to go."

"But you do." Tippy let her cheek rest for a fleeting moment against the comforting haven of his chest, then led the way to the car.

"I wasn't crying about that," she repeated, when they were side by side on the hot, uncomfortable seat. "I shed streams of tears over that long ago, when you first got your orders." She gave him a smile that, although wan, was reassuring, as those of service wives need to be. "My only question, sir," she said, trying to sound light, "is this: Do we have to sell our house to the Pattersons?"

"Why, darling, we decided we will," he answered, looking at her in surprise while he let the car find its own way along the familiar driveway. "You can't stay out here in these woods alone. Had I gone last year when I thought I was going, my kid sister would have come down and lived with you. But now that Bitsy is a successful up-and-coming author, she wants to stay in New York."

"The Johnstons are right next door," Tippy protested, trying not to notice how sparsely settled the quiet country road was.

"But they close up and go away for six months of the year." Peter was watching for his chance to move out onto the crowded highway, and when he was safely in the swiftly moving traffic, he asked, "What brought on this sudden change? Just last night we decided that we'd sell out, and you'd go up near West Point where we have dozens of relatives."

"I don't want to be dependent on our families," Tippy protested, her narrow shoulders straight against the back of the seat. "Mums and Dad have a nice little house. It's darling, but it's small—too small for me to crowd into with the children. Of course, David and Carrol have an enormous mansion on their estate where we could have the guest wing and nobody would have to see us unless they wanted too. Penny and Josh have a good-sized house on Round Tree Farm, but they're going out to Hollywood while Penny makes a movie. Maybe they'll take Parri and Joshu with them, but most likely they won't. Penny wrote in her last letter that she hopes Parri will want to stay home and run the house. She thinks it will be good for her, so I'm not going there to take over her responsibility. As for your father . . ." she turned and looked at him before she said ". . . he's reared eight children and now he deserves to have his home in peace. Bobby and Susan?" She stopped and gave a small shudder before she said, "Bobby would drive me mad. He would try to run my life. He always did when we were little and he hasn't changed. I don't want to go back and camp around with the family, Peter. Not for one year or perhaps for the two you may have to put in."

"Gosh, I understand how you feel." They were approaching the motel where the Pattersons were staying temporarily; and parking beside its office, he cut his motor and said miserably, "Let's sit here a few minutes and talk this over. It won't hurt the Pattersons to wait a little longer. They know they'll get our house or one they don't like as well, and I can't worry about them. It's you I'm worried about."

"Thank you," Tippy said in a small voice. Then she listened to him go on:

"I thought it was all settled that we'd sell our house and you'd take the equity we have in it to buy something up near our folks, or rent something if you prefer to. Was I right?"

"Yes, you were," Tippy conceded, because last night she had had no one but herself and her children to consider. Now she had Marny. She had to stay in Atlanta so she could help Marny. Some way, she had to move Marny from the Bullocks to the Jordons. She had to take care of Marny.

"Okay," she listened to Peter point out with his matter-of-fact mind, "you have lots of friends in Atlanta, but not close ones. Up in New York, you've got a family that cares about you, so why should you suddenly want to stay in Atlanta?"

"It's Marny," Tippy blurted out. And there in the hot August sunshine, in the wilting heat that rose from the spongy asphalt, she told him the story of Marny's pitiful life. "I can't abandon her," she said at the end. "Yesterday I could have because I didn't know about her. Today I can't. Someone has to look after Marny. No one else,

34

except perhaps Miss Wilcox, is trying to, so I'll have to be the one. I think God means me to be," she said softly. "He gave me Tippy Two and Petey, and now He's entrusting Marny to me. He's given her to me as a trust, Peter."

"Oh, darling." Peter couldn't tell the dedicated girl beside him that state and county laws governed Marny, that the Children's Welfare, working in Marny's interest, had placed her with the Bullocks. Tippy wouldn't buy that. Neither would she settle for a promise to Marny that after she reached eighteen the Jordons and the Parrishes would see that she got to college. He could only explain with clear, logical reasoning, "There may not be anything we can do right now, Tip. I feel awfully sorry for Marny, too, and perhaps I can understand her predicament better than you can. I was only fourteen when my stepmother died and Dad had to go off to war. He dumped all eight of us in a boxy little house in Florida. We had to. . . ."

"But you had brothers and sisters with you," Tippy interrupted. "Marny hasn't anybody."

"I know that." Peter thought of Jenifer who at sixteen had held the abandoned little family together. Marny's present life couldn't be much worse than Jenifer's had been, but he said, "You've got to think of me, too."

"You?" Tippy asked, looking at him in surprise.

"Yes, me. I'm your husband. I'm ordered to Vietnam. I have to go. I'm willing and I want to, but I can't go that far away and do a good job with half my mind worrying about you here in Atlanta, out in the woods alone. I'd be worried sick."

"I wouldn't want to worry you, Peter, darling." Tippy flung her arms about him, not caring that the manager of the motel was watching them curiously through a side win-

35

dow. "I couldn't do that to you." Then, still holding him, she leaned back to say, "Do you think I can take Marny with me?"

"Tippy, I don't know." He loved her so much. Her dearness, her sweetness, her gaiety, her loving heart that always made her bring home stray animals that she spent days finding homes for.

"I can try," Tippy said into his silence. "I think the Children's Welfare Society would be glad for Marny to find a happy home with young parents, even if one of them will have to go away to war. And if it does approve, I'll hustle to find a house near our family. Marny can help me run things and you won't have to worry about me."

"And if it doesn't approve?" Peter had to ask.

"I'll cross that bridge when I come to it." Tippy turned her little chin into something resembling a determined jaw. "Now, I guess we'd better go in and tell the Pattersons that they can have our precious house," she said, smoothing her green cotton dress and picking up her purse. "How soon will we have to give it to them?"

"In ten days." Peter knew he looked hot and wrinkled, but it didn't matter. He had begun to hope that this business of Marny would take Tippy's mind off the sad business of moving; so he said, "My orders were cut today. They give me time to clear out everything here and have almost three weeks' leave. We should get where we're going and have you settled somewhere by then."

He opened the door on his side; but as she still sat in silence, he closed it again to listen to her say, "Peter, can we afford to stay in a motel when we get home? In Highland Falls, perhaps? I don't like to be beholden."

"Why, I guess we can, Tip, if that's what you want." He

leaned across the wheel to kiss her cheek that slipped away from his lips because she was nodding with satisfaction.

"I've been married too long to want to be beholden," she said. "We'd only need two rooms, because Marny and Tippy Two and Petey can room together. That way, we'll be free to do as we like."

So far as Tippy was concerned, Marny was going with them. Peter prayed that neither of them would be disappointed.

"I don't think we should tell Marny yet," she was saying, as he came around the car to open her door. "I'll go talk to Mrs. Bullock first thing tomorrow morning, then Miss Wilcox."

"But what if Marny doesn't want to go?" he had to ask.

"Oh, she will." Tippy was confident and smiling as they knocked on the door of Number 8.

Captain Patterson opened the door, and for a moment Peter was afraid he would have to push Tippy inside. Then she squared her shoulders like a good soldier to say, "You can have our house. We've decided. Peter thinks I should go somewhere near our relatives. He says he can't go off to war worrying about me and the children, so I'll have to do whatever will be easiest for him. That is. . . ." She was about to add her one reservation, that of taking Marny, but Peter was already making definite plans.

"Could you good people stick it out here for ten days longer?" he asked.

"Oh, we'd manage," Mrs. Patterson answered quickly, turning back from boosting up the air conditioner. "Your house is the only one in our price range that appeals to us."

The Pattersons were a couple Tippy had thought she

would like to know if she stayed on in Atlanta, but now that she was committed to move, she was in a great hurry to scoop up Marny, and leave.

She chattered all the way home about the new life she would give Marny and what a help Marny would be to her. And even though Peter warned her that a state has strict laws governing its orphans, she refused to accept it.

"I'll work it out," she told him confidently. "I'm sure that whoever is responsible for Marny will want her to be happy. I like her so much that I'll simply have to help straighten out her life. I'll have to, Peter. Why, just suppose," she turned on the seat to say, "something should happen to you and me, and there would be no one to look after Tippy Two and Petey!"

"That couldn't happen." Peter sent her a wry but encouraging smile. "Not in our big families. The kids would have a dozen uncles and aunts to take over."

"Ten, actually," she corrected. "No, six—because I wouldn't let Bobby have them, and Jenifer lives 'way off in England."

"Well, six should do it, and we still have your parents and my father in reserve." Then, to divert her mind from a possible parental demise, he said, "Start your ball rolling. If you can work it to take Marny with us, it's fine with me."

He didn't know what she planned to do with Marny when he came back from Vietnam and the War Department decided to send them heaven alone knew where, but that wasn't an immediate problem. Tippy's present happiness was—and Marny's, of course. If Marny could give Tippy something to look forward to, if she could provide an incentive for the long days and nights of his absence, he would be forever grateful to her. "Have a go at it," he said. "I'll back you up whenever you need me."

Tippy hopped out before the car had quite settled on its wheels in the driveway. "Marny? Marny?" She called eagerly, jerking open the front door and listening for the sound of voices.

"We're in here, Mrs. Jordon," Marny answered from the kitchen; and Tippy raced through the small dining room.

Quite a sight met her eyes. Two ladies and a gentleman were having tea around Tippy Two's little play table. The smaller lady wore a dress of her mother's and a flower hat; the larger one, whose knees were doubled up almost under her chin, was completely enveloped in a ruffled kitchen apron; the wee gentleman had on his father's golf cap and plaid gardening shirt.

"Oh, Marny," Tippy cried, as the beruffled maid jumped up from the table in such a rush that milk spilled out of the tiny cups, "do you think Mrs. Bullock will let you spend the night here? I have an early appointment tomorrow and I can't take the children with me."

"Why, yes, I'm sure she would," Marny answered, while Tippy lifted the flower hat and the golf cap to bend down and kiss the tops of her children's heads. "She and Mr. Bullock are going to a party tonight, so I'm sure they'll be glad to let me stay."

"Then run telephone them!" Tippy looked at the damage she had caused and at Tippy Two, who had risen to point to it, and was saying in a distressed ladylike voice, quite different from her usual shrill pipe, "You ruined our party. Just look at this mess."

"I'm sorry, darling, but I'm arranging it so you can have another playtime tomorrow. Why don't you give Major Jordon a piece of your delicious-looking cake?" she added, as Peter came in through the kitchen door. "I'd join you but I have to go check on Mrs. Bullock's answer." And out she darted, leaving Peter to cope with Tippy Two's indignant mopping up.

"Thank you, Mrs. Bullock," Marny was saying when Tippy reached the living room, and she added, "Good-by." She was smiling when she replaced the receiver of the telephone that stood on a table beside the stairway. To spend the night in the Jordons' lovely guest room was a delight to her. She had slept there twice, and each time had pretended it belonged to her. "I do love to stay here," she said shyly.

"Well, maybe you can. . . ." Tippy jerked her thoughts into control the way she sometimes had to slam on Old Betsy's brakes, and sat down. "Do you think you could call me Aunt Tippy?" she found herself asking. "Mrs. Jordon sounds so formal. I know I'm lots older than you are," she said, as Marny looked startled. "I'm not old enough to be your mother, but I could be an aunt. Could you manage to say Aunt Tippy and Uncle Peter?"

"I—why, I don't know." Marny sat down, too. She sat in a paper-doll collapse onto the little chair beside the telephone table. "I could try, Mrs. Jordon—I mean, well, I could try if you want me to. But you won't be here very much longer," she reminded. "Tippy Two told me that you're leaving Atlanta soon and. . . ."

"I know we are," Tippy interrupted, "but I'd like to have you stay here all the time while we're packing. I'll be so busy that I won't have time to look after the children, and I thought if Mrs. Bullock would let you, I'd keep you right here." It was a lame explanation for the aunt-and-uncle bit, since Marny could only assume that she would never see the Jordons again after they left Atlanta, but Tippy was sure she could clarify it in just a few days. "It would be a terrific help to me," she added.

"It would?"

Marny's face came so alive with pleasure that Tippy found herself tiptoeing through mined territory as she asked, "Do you like to stay with us, Marny?"

"Oh, I love to. I love you all. Sometimes," Marny said wistfully, "I feel as if you're the family I might have had if Mother and Daddy had lived, and I could have had a little sister and brother. I pretend that."

"Go right on pretending." Tippy clamped her lips together as she saw Peter come through the dining room. She was the one who had cautioned against raising a false hope in Marny, yet here she was about to blurt out their plan. Somehow, Peter always managed to save her from her own indiscretions.

"I'd better go dress for the cookout now," she said, standing up. "Everything is ready for your and the children's supper, Marny. All you have to do is warm the spaghetti and meatballs and remember to wake Switzy from his nap and feed him."

"Yes, Mrs. Jordon, I'll do everything."

Tippy watched Peter disappear at the top of the stairway, and sure he couldn't hear her, she said, "What did you say, Marny?"

"I said, Yes, Mrs. Jordon, I can do it."

41

"Were you speaking to me?" Tippy looked so blank that Marny smiled and forced herself to say, "Yes, Aunt Tippy."

Then, unexpectedly, in a mingle of blond hair and brown, they were hugging each other.

3

Marny, waking in the blue-and-white room, was still unable to believe her good fortune. She was to spend ten whole days with the Jordons! She could say "Aunt Tippy" fairly easily now, because she had practiced it all the evening before, but Major Jordon was still Major Jordon to her and she had managed to look directly at him whenever she addressed him. Ten whole days of bliss lay before her.

She hopped out from between the percale sheets that felt soft as silk and stood before the mirror. It was a big, clear mirror above a dressing table, and it gave back a happy girl in a pink nightgown that was as short and full as the party dress she had made yesterday for Tippy Two's paper doll.

It was only seven o'clock and the house was quiet, but she tiptoed into the bathroom she shared with the Jordon children, used the new toothbrush she had been given the night before, and dressed quickly. Her blue dress wasn't as fresh as she would have liked it to be, and her hair, after a free night without rollers, was even more stubborn than usual, but she had no time to worry about such defects. She wanted to be downstairs and have breakfast ready when the others came down.

From her two previous overnight visits, she knew the Jordons ate in the breakfast area every morning, so she laid placemats and silver on the table, poured orange juice into glasses and set them in the refrigerator, whisking about the kitchen, humming softly and happily. The percolater was bubbling a tune with her when Tippy came in.

"Why, Marny Alexander, you sweet child," Tippy said, surprised to find the most confusing part of her day taken care of. "I feel as if I should have drifted in in my laciest negligee."

"You could go back and put it on," Marny suggested eagerly, but Tippy shook her head.

"Not today," she said, as she fastened a chain belt around her white sleeveless dress. "I have too many errands to do. While I'm out," she went on, watching Marny set a glass of chilled orange juice on the table, "I'll stop by Mrs. Bullock's and ask her to pack a suitcase for you. Thank you, sugar."

Marny was back at the counter now, pouring coffee into a flowered china cup, and because Tippy knew it would please her, she made a great show of sitting down at the table and giving a gusty sigh of pleasure. "I don't know myself in this rich state," she said, quirking her little finger with exaggerated elegance as she lifted the glass.

Marny wanted to ask if she would like to have her toast now, but found it hard to bring out the Aunt Tippy so early in the morning. It was like learning to swim, she thought. You went to the pool in the high school gym for the first time, and you did pretty well with an instructor holding you up. Then you went back the next day to do it alone, and you sank. She decided to make the toast, then serve it.

"Look, sugar," Tippy said, watching Marny's quick, deft movements, "aren't you coming over to have breakfast with me? It's no fun eating alone. I snatch a cup of coffee every morning while I'm getting ready for the onslaught, so let's be sociable. I'm letting your Uncle Peter sleep late today," she went on chattily, as Marny brought the coffee and slid into a chair, "because Mimi Patterson is coming out to do some measuring and offered to drop him off at his office if I'm late coming back with the car."

When Marny heard "your Uncle Peter" near panic seized her. She was to be left here with Major Jordon. She couldn't stare at him when she wanted to speak to him, or poke him to attract his attention. She decided that she would have to go right on calling him Major Jordon. Sitting alone with Tippy at the table, there would be no difficulty. She could simply say "you." But before six sentences had been exchanged, Tippy Two and Petey flung themselves into the kitchen as if they were starving, and both she and Tippy became short-order cooks.

"Oh, golly, I've got to go!" Tippy exclaimed, when the two intruders were spooning up cereal with their eyes on the stove, where Marny was frying bacon. "Petey, go wake

45

your father. Tippy Two, bring me my purse from the living room. No, wait a minute," she called as they both raced past her. "I want to remind you that you're in Marny's charge today. Daddy will be busy with Mrs. Patterson, and after they leave you're to mind Marny. Do you get that?"

They said they did; and after Petey had shouted "Daddy, get up" from every step of the stairway and Tippy Two had brought the white purse, she looked about the kitchen that had been reduced to its usual morning shambles, and said, "I'll have to go. I really will if I'm to attend to everything I have to do." Then she asked Marny, "Can you take care of this mess I'm leaving you?"

"Of course I can," Marny answered staunchly. "There isn't much to do."

"Well, then, I'm off." Tippy rummaged in her purse for her car keys, and halfway out the door she called back, "Good-by, dears."

"Good-by, Mums," Tippy Two and Petey caroled together, while Marny said only a quick "Good-by."

"Good-by, who?" Tippy paused long enough to ask.

"Good-by, Aunt Tippy." Marny's words were shy and murmured, but Petey threw his arms around her waist, and, climbing up like a monkey, repeated them shrilly.

My goodness, what an ill-behaved child, Tippy thought pleasantly, riding along in the morning air that was already becoming hot. Then she frowned and asked herself distractedly, "What did I do with the map Peter drew for me that shows a short cut to the Bullocks'? He's taken Marny home lots of times, and he showed me how to keep from driving in town and out again."

She reached a stop light that obligingly turned red for

her, and rummaged about in her purse until she came up with a piece of paper that showed Peter's directions. Two cars honked at her before she was ready to move on again, so she held the paper against the steering wheel while she tried to find the diagonal road he had marked. By some good fortune she eventually turned onto a street that was lined with weary brick houses, and saw Number 1486 just ahead of her.

No one answered her ring after she had climbed disabled steps and repeatedly punched a bell under a card that had BULLOCK printed on it, so she peeked in a window. A living room, so far as she could see through mesh fiber-glass curtains, was empty, and she went back to ring again. She rang several times before she decided to follow a narrow cement walk around the house and try the kitchen door. She was sure it was too early for Mrs. Bullock to have left home, and, pushing open a white sagging gate, she saw her. Mrs. Bullock was pinning sheets to a clothesline in the back yard.

"Good gracious, you gave me a start," she said, when Tippy appeared on the sparse, sunburned grass. "I didn't know anyone was within fifty feet of me."

"I'm Andrea Jordon," Tippy said hastily. "I came to talk to you about Marny."

"Oh, yes, you're the lady she baby-sits for." Mrs. Bullock took a clothespin from the capacious pocket of her apron and nipped it onto the corner of a limp, wet sheet. "Every time she comes from your house all she can talk about is the Jordons: what they did, what they said, and how they looked. She almost talks my ear off. She's a nice little girl, Marny."

Tippy saw her opportunity and moved right in by saying, "We think she's a love. My husband is an army officer and is ordered to Vietnam so we're going to leave Atlanta. I'm taking the children up to New York State, to live near my family, and we want Marny to go with us. Do you think she can?"

"You want to take Marny? Oh, for goodness' sake!" Mrs. Bullock untied her apron and dropped it into the clothes-basket before she said, "I don't know if the law will let you."

"Would you have any objection?" Tippy asked.

"No." Mrs. Bullock shook her head, then said, "As I told you, Marny's a nice girl as girls go, and not much trouble. I never wanted to take in older children. Babies are easier, but I've done the best by her that I can."

"I know you have," Tippy put in quickly. "Marny says that this is the best place she has lived since her grand-mother died."

"I don't know about that, but she's been looked after." Mrs. Bullock picked up her basket, and, resting it on her hip, asked, "What makes you young folks want to take her with you?"

"We've come to love her," Tippy answered truthfully, "and we want to help her. I coaxed her to tell me about her pitiful life before she came here to you, and the minute she finished, I knew I was meant to be the next one to help her—and she was meant to be a comfort to me while Peter is away. I have a big family up in New York, Mrs. Bullock, a great big wonderful family who will love Marny. She deserves a lot of love. I thought, if you will give me some of her clothes, she could stay out at our house."

"Let's go inside and talk about it. I'm willing for Marny to go," Mrs. Bullock said, leading the way, "but you don't seem to understand that you can't just pick up a ward of the state and make off with her."

"Oh, but I do," Tippy protested, following along to a narrow back porch where Mrs. Bullock set the basket on a splint-bottomed chair and they squeezed past a defunct refrigerator and a stepladder to enter a kitchen that was surprisingly modern and smelled of disinfectant. "I knew the first move to make was to ask you how you felt about giving up Marny, then hope you could tell me what to do next."

"It won't be easy." Mrs. Bullock led the way through a dining room that looked as if it was seldom used and into a living room filled with heavy furniture, upholstered in dark red mohair. "I'd better warn you that it won't," she said, turning on an electric fan to stir up hot air around their feet. "Sit down."

Tippy chose a chair directly in front of the fan. She wanted to ask how she should start the wheels moving, but Mrs. Bullock was leaning back against the prickly upholstery, mopping her face and looking thoughtful. "I guess Miss Wilcox can advise you better than I can," she said at last, shaking the front of her dress to let more air reach her bulky body. "Doris Wilcox—although she doesn't have much say about anything, being just a caseworker—knows I don't really want Marny and that it's awfully hard for me and my husband to stay home all the time and keep track of her, now that she goes gallivanting off to evening classes. Last night was pure pleasure because we got to go out without worrying about leaving Marny here alone."

"Where would I find Miss Wilcox?" Tippy asked, glad

the Bullocks had had a pleasant evening but not wanting to dwell on the inconvenience that housing Marny caused them.

"She has an office downtown somewhere, but she's usually off making her investigating trips. I don't think you could reach her there. She goes to the hospitals, and she goes to people's houses to check on how the children she placed there are doing. She's a busy woman. She's always on the go."

"I'd like to try," Tippy replied promptly, to cut off a recital of Miss Wilcox's many activities. "Perhaps I could make an appointment with her. I don't have much time," she explained. "Just ten days—nine, really, because we have to be out of the house on the tenth day."

"I have her telephone number and you can call her from here if you like," Mrs. Bullock suggested, reluctantly heaving herself away from the fan's cooling reach. "Didn't you say you wanted me to pack some clothes for Marny?"

"Yes, please."

"Then I'll do it while you make your call. You've got the phone right there on that table beside you and you can find the number in the flip-up directory. Just move the needle down to W."

"Thank you."

Tippy could hear Mrs. Bullock grunting on every step of the steep enclosed stairway, and was sure that she rarely went up to visit Marny's quarters. A neat downstairs bedroom was visible beyond the living room, and she assumed that the nursery was beside it and opening into the sterile kitchen. She pulled the telephone pad toward her, moved its indicator to W as she had been instructed to do, and jumped when its lid flew up, exposing Miss Wilcox's number written in red ink. To her surprise the voice that answered her said, "Welfare, Children's Division, Miss Wilcox speaking."

"Oh, Miss Wilcox, I'm Andrea Jordon, and I'm calling about helping Marny," Tippy gasped out, both from surprise and nervousness. "Could I see you right away?"

Doris Wilcox failed to grasp the meaning of the call. It took several minutes to make her understand at least a part of it; and Mrs. Bullock was back with Marny's meager summer wardrobe packed in a small wicker hamper by the time Tippy had scribbled the number of a downtown building on the rumpled map Peter had made and was telling the perplexed woman on the other end of the line that she would be in her office in twenty minutes.

"This is all I could find to put her clothes in," Mrs. Bullock said apologetically, setting the hamper by the door. "If you're going to keep Marny for a while, Mr. Bullock will take me on one of his selling trips with him, and I'll need my suitcase."

"Oh, this will be fine," Tippy assured her, edging toward the door. "Will you be gone long? I mean, if we should need you for filling out papers?"

"Just a few days. We'll be back by Saturday. I may go again, though, if I don't get a baby in. I like to ride around to different towns."

"I'll call you on Saturday. Thank you, Mrs. Bullock, you've been a great help to me, and I know Marny will appreciate it, everything you've done, too," Tippy said gratefully, snatching up the hamper and letting herself out into a blast of heat.

"Well, give her my regards and tell her I want the best for her." Mrs. Bullock closed the door and said to herself, thinking of Marny, "I hope something good turns out for her."

To Tippy's joy, Miss Wilcox's office was air-conditioned. Miss Wilcox was a sweet-looking woman in her early forties. She had nice blue eyes and tan hair with streaks of gray in it. Meeting her, Tippy liked her at once.

"What was it you were telling me about Marny?" she asked, when she was sitting at her desk with Tippy in a comfortable chair beside her. "It sounded as if you're planning to abduct her."

"Oh, it isn't quite like that," Tippy answered, smiling. And she launched into the explanation that she had rehearsed while she drove downtown. "That's the way it is," she said when she finished. "Marny needs us and we want Marny. Do you think you can help us get her to live with us?"

They talked for an hour; and when Tippy left the office her mind was so filled with statistics and the rules and regulations governing a ward of the state, that she couldn't remember which parking meter was guarding her car.

"I've never had a case like this," Miss Wilcox had said at the door, "so I have no precedent to go by. Adoptive parents can take a child wherever they please, but foster parents—Mrs. Jordon, I don't think they can."

"But you do think it would be good for Marny to go with us, don't you?" Tippy queried anxiously.

"Yes, if your credentials are acceptable in both Georgia and New York, I'd love for Marny to go. Let me talk to my immediate superior and perhaps he can bring it up before the board. It meets day after tomorrow, and I'll call you just as soon as I have a decision," she promised. "I'll tell you whatever news I receive, good or bad." And with that, Tippy had to be content.

"So that's the way it is," she said to Peter on the telephone, when, hot and tired, she reached home. "I've decided to tell Marny what we're doing. I think, if she is going with us, she ought to know and have time to be happy and excited about it."

"But, Tippy," he protested, "you don't *know*, yet, that she is going."

"Oh, she is," Tippy answered confidently. "I think what is right is right, and nothing can stop it. It's right for Marny to go. It's right for her to be happy, and nothing—not anything—can block it. I'm sure of that, Peter, so you be sure of it, too." Then she replaced the receiver and called upstairs to Marny.

"Stop pampering those children and tell them to lie down and rest," she shouted. "Tell them their mother is hot and tired and wants you to come down to sit with her while she eats a late lunch. And give them a kiss for me," she remembered to add. "I'd come up but I'm bushed."

"Oh, Aunt Tippy," Marny cried, when she ran into the kitchen to find Tippy leaning against the counter, pouring iced tea down her throat, "if I had known when you'd be home I'd have saved some lunch for you."

"It doesn't matter." Tippy was cooling off now. Her dress was coming loose from her back and she had kicked off her high-heeled pumps.

She watched while Marny took a package of cold boiled ham from the refrigerator; then, opening the lid of the breadbox, she pulled out two slices of bread and held them out, saying, "Slap the ham between these and I'll be fine. I have to talk to you about something important, sugar, so let's go in the living room where I can put up my feet, and relax."

She padded through the dining room, taking large bites from her sandwich and washing them down with iced tea, then settled herself on the sofa. Marny sat across the coffee table from her, and they were posed exactly as they had been yesterday when their fateful conversation had begun.

"Marny," Tippy said, not bothering about how to start off, "your Uncle Peter and I want to take you up north with us. Would you like to go?"

"Oh, Aunt Tippy, you can't *mean* it!" Marny slid off her chair and walked on her knees across the space that separated them.

"Yes, I do. We're very serious about it."

"You *are?*" she cried, sitting back with her legs doubled under her. "*You really are?*"

"I was never more serious in my life." Tippy gulped down the last bite of her sandwich and followed it with the last of her iced tea, then held out the glass to Marny. "Hick-hick," she hiccuped, after trying to swallow something that was too large to slide down. "There, it's gone. We want you to live with us, darling," she said, sitting up and taking Marny's cheeks between her hands. "That's what I've been arranging all morning. First I went to see Mrs. Bullock; then I went to see Miss Wilcox. Do you think you'd like to, Marny?"

"Oh, Aunt Tippy!" Both Marny's face and the glass were buried in Tippy's lap. "Oh, I'm so happy, I'm so happy," she sobbed over and over.

"There, sugar, don't cry." Tippy had expected joy, but not tears with it, so she gently released Marny's hold on the

54

glass and smoothed back her hair. "I would have broken the news more slowly," she said, as the sobs subsided, "if I'd known it was going to knock you out. This is no time, sugar, for crying."

"I know it." Marny swallowed a few more sobs and looked up to ask, "Aunt Tippy, are you sure I can go?"

"Of course I'm sure." Tippy was. There would be a few papers to sign and an investigation of her and Peter's reliability, but she was certain that anyone who had charge of Marny's welfare was bound to see what a marvelous opportunity this would be for her. She had no doubts about it.

Marny herself was afraid to believe it. Nothing this good had happened to her in eleven years. Someone truly wanted her at last! The realization was so blinding that she blinked as if she had come from darkness into sudden bright daylight. "Does Uncle Major want me?" she asked, still not quite able to bring out Peter's new name.

"Uncle Major thinks it's wonderful," Tippy answered, chuckling at Marny's compromise with Peter's title. "When he comes home he'll tell you so and we'll have a celebration." Then, to break the tension, she cried, "Oh, Marny, we have so much to do! We must start packing the good linens and blankets and winter clothes; and when the movers bring us some big cartons, we'll begin on the books. And we'll have shopping and marketing to do, because no matter how busy we are we have to eat."

There was the usual afternoon sound of running feet above them, and although it was fifteen minutes too early, Tippy, after giving Marny a hasty kiss on her wet cheek, leaned around her to call, "Come on down, kids. We have a surprise for you."

Petey, dragging his T-shirt, appeared on the stairway

55

with his boxer shorts on crooked, and Tippy Two hurried behind him, the back of her dress unbuttoned. "Are we going to have ice cream?" Tippy Two shouted, racing around Petey so she could back up to Marny for help.

"We can, but that isn't the surprise," Tippy answered, watching Marny slide around on the carpet and become busy with the buttons. "Marny is going to be your new cousin, just like Davy and Lang and Parri and Carli and Ti Me are, and little Jonathan down in Pennsylvania."

"How?" Petey inquired matter-of-factly, standing with his hands on his hips and looking as skeptical as his father had sounded on the telephone. "How can she be a cousin when she wasn't born one?"

"By our declaring her to be one and taking her to live with us forever and ever."

"Oh, I'm so glad!" Tippy Two cried, twisting around to fling herself at Marny and almost upsetting them both. "We can play paper dolls and have tea parties every day."

"And we can play baseball, too," Petey grunted, as his mother jerked his shorts around to hang straight.

"That's where you're both wrong," Tippy told him, giving his fat little bottom a spank as she released him. "We're going to be a busy family, getting ready to move."

"But I can play *sometimes*," Marny consoled them, seeing their disappointment. "When we haven't anything important to do, we can play."

Petey began capering about, but Tippy Two looked thoughtful as she turned her gaze on her mother. "Did Marny know about this yesterday when she started calling you Aunt Tippy?" she asked.

"No," Tippy answered, shaking her head. "Daddy and I

did, or hoped we did, so I asked her to call me Aunt Tippy. Now she says Uncle Major, too."

Petey stopped in the middle of a roll across the floor to ask, "Uncle *Major*—who's he?"

"He's Daddy. Marny has always called him Major, and now she's added the Uncle to it."

"That's a crazy name."

He continued his rolling, but Tippy Two tossed her head and told him, "I think it's nice and respectful. Daddy's an army officer, you jerk. He expects you to say 'sir' when you answer him, 'yes, sir,' 'no, sir,' and I've been thinking that perhaps it would sound more military if I called him 'Daddy, sir.'"

"Oh, you silly children." Tippy jumped up from the sofa, and raced to the kitchen. She had heard a car pull into the driveway, and she wanted to be the first to tell Peter that she had already broken the good news to Marny.

"Tippy Jordon, you've gone and told her!" he said, his first words erasing some of the joy from the bright face he had just kissed. "You shouldn't have done that, yet. I talked to the mayor after the civic meeting we just had, and he didn't sound very hopeful."

"Oh, the *mayor*," Tippy scoffed. "What does he know about orphaned children! He just runs the city—its money and things. I have *interested* people working for us."

"Dear Lord, I hope you have." Peter followed her through the dining room and grinned at Marny, who still sat on the floor as if too paralyzed to get up. Now she scrambled to her feet and watched Petey and Tippy Two fling themselves at him. "Hey, there, kids, take it easy," he said, breaking loose from the arms that entwined him so he could toss his necktie on a chair. "Welcome to the fold, Marny. The old man is too bushed to say more."

"Thank you, Uncle Major," Marny answered quickly, trying out the new name with experimental hesitance. "I'll get you some lemonade," and she darted for the kitchen.

Tippy Two and Petey followed her as if lured by a feminine Pied Piper, and Peter turned to Tippy with a quizzical, worried look. "Gosh, I hope you haven't made a mistake, Tip," he said.

"I haven't." Tippy was still sure that Marny would be able to go with them, but not quite as sure as she had been before Peter's reported conversation with the mayor. "You don't think I have, do you?" she asked.

"I don't know. From what I heard today there's a lot of red tape entailed in taking a ward out of the state. Nobody here has ever tried it, Tippy."

"Well, we are now," Tippy returned, her mouth so tight that the dimple bored in. "This state has never run up against the combination of a Parrish and a Jordon," she declared, thinking of her father's military record and of General Jordon who had been an indomitable foe in the Second World War. "When we go into battle, we win."

"Okay," Peter agreed, sitting down beside her and pulling her against him. "Where do we attack, Madam Commander of the United Armies?"

"I don't know." Tippy had to admit that nothing could be done until she heard from Miss Wilcox, who was only a small cog in the state's machinery. "We can make our plans day after tomorrow when we hear what the board has to say. In the meantime, tomorrow," she said, "we go to Miss Wilcox's office and sign a paper—a petition for custody, I guess you'd call it. It will give our background and qualifications for becoming foster parents of one Marian Alexander."

"Okay, what time?"

"As early as we can get there, I guess," Tippy answered vaguely.

"Six o'clock? Seven? We can make it by then."

"After nine o'clock, silly," she told him scathingly. "Miss Wilcox won't be in her office until nine."

"Nine o'clock it is then, on the dot." He hugged her shoulders that were still tense with worry, and said, "We'll swear to our good intentions and offer all our worldly goods, of which we have none, at nine o'clock sharp."

A parade was marching in from the dining room, and Tippy Two's shrill pipe announced, "You have lemonade, Daddy, and we all have ice cream and Girl Scout cookies."

"Don't lose your courage, Childie," he found time to whisper, "no matter how high the odds are stacked against us. We're in there fighting, and we know that no battle was ever won by indecisive faltering."

4

Three members of the Jordon family had difficulty going to sleep that night. Tippy, lying with her eyes wide open and staring at the ceiling, was making a mental list of all she had to do in the days to come. Peter, wakeful in his half of the king-sized bed, was on constant alert to answer the whisper that came out of the dark.

"Who do you think we should give for character references besides our minister?" it asked once.

"The Cartrights, they're our best friends," he answered promptly, having already considered and settled that question himself. "And Colonel James and our folks up home."

"Thank you." The voice was quiet for all of five minutes. Then it asked again, "When the movers take out the furniture on the day before we leave, what are we going to sleep on?"

"Go to a motel, I guess," he said, but the voice disputed that.

"It would be too hard," it said. "We can't move and clean the house and pack the car all in one day."

"Then I'll get folding cots from the National Guard." Peter had studied that problem, too. "Jim Patterson," he said, "will return them after we leave."

"I'll keep out one sheet apiece, and I can buy instant coffee and leave out a couple of my oldest pans."

Ten whole minutes passed before Tippy wakened him from a vague, shimmering little dream that was just beginning to drift hazily through his semiconsciousness. "Do you really have to go to Fort Benning on Thursday?" he heard her ask.

"Um-hum," he roused himself to answer. "On the early plane. I'll come back on a late one Friday."

"Oh, dear, what if I need you in the meantime?"

Her voice was plaintively near, so he knew she was leaning over him. "I'll sign every paper they shove at me tomorrow and I'll pull all the strings I can," he promised.

"Will you talk to the mayor again?"

"I can't, Tip. He left right after the meeting today for a month's vacation."

"Oh-h-h-h." A sigh brushed his cheek when she dropped back again, but her voice went on, "If something should come up," it asked, "could you fly home earlier?"

"There's not a chance of that, Childie. You see," he turned to her to explain, as he had done a few days before when the order came in, "I went down to Florida last year and took that gosh-awful survival course when I thought I was going to Vietnam. I don't have to go through another two weeks of that agony, but I will get a lot of briefing on it and on my job with troops. I don't want to go to Benning, darling, but I have to."

"I know that." Tippy sighed acceptantly, then asked, "You'll be home in time for the party Colonel and Mrs. James are giving for us on Friday, won't you? It's to be a farewell for us and a welcome to the Pattersons."

"I'll make it," he promised.

"It's to be at the country club and is to start at five o'clock," she went on, as if talking reassuringly to herself, "so we can leave early and get home before dark. The Cartrights' party on Saturday is an informal affair, and Audrey said to bring the kids and Marny, so that will work out all right."

There was another short silence before he heard her murmur, "I suppose we'd better go to sleep now. If we don't, I'll look like such a hag tomorrow that Miss Wilcox's boss won't think I'm fit to have Marny. Good night, Peter dear."

"Good night, Childie." Silence, with only the faint sound of even breathing, took over.

Marny, in the room that was almost hers, was too excited to sleep. She sat before the window, looking out at the beautiful moonlit night and wondering how she would feel when such loveliness truly became hers. Doubts had begun to creep in and fear that nothing so wonderful could happen to Marny Alexander. "I mustn't worry," she tried to reassure herself, "because Aunt Tippy promised that it would, and when Uncle Major told me good night, he said, 'It will be nice to have a niece of our own, one that we don't have to share with the rest of the family.' *They* believe it."

Marny tried to, too. And when the moon was sliding lower in the sky, she dropped to her knees before the window and offered a simple, thankful prayer to God for His loving, tender care of her. Then she slipped into her cool bed and went gratefully to sleep.

A busy week followed. It was a week of both hurry and waiting. The first morning had passed with Peter and Tippy stating their desire to become foster parents, having interviews and signing papers. Then, unexpectedly, Marny was needed. Her wishes must be consulted; her desire to live with the Jordons in another state must be verified, put in writing, and signed by her.

Peter drove home for her, leaving Tippy to telephone an advance warning and to tell her that Tippy Two and Petey, for lack of a second baby sitter, would have to come with her. "Don't let them start their rest period," Tippy said. "Just see that they're clean and presentable. Nobody's going to notice them—and, oh, Marny, everything is moving along just fine!"

Marny, with stifled excitement, sat in a Mr. Bosserman's office, the shy little star of the show, making simple concise statements about her past that filled Tippy's heart with pride and sometimes brought tears to her eyes. "She had an unhappy childhood," Mr. Bosserman, the head of the Welfare Department, agreed. And at a question from Peter he added, "Yes, I do think she deserves a chance."

The family returned home feeling triumphant. But that was only the first day. After the flush of victory was over, the waiting began. Peter flew off on his official trip to Fort

Benning; the Hallaran Moving and Storage Company delivered large cardboard cartons that Tippy and Marny filled with blankets and winter clothes, while the children tossed in the old but precious toys they couldn't bear to discard. Tippy's friends popped in at intervals because she refused to leave the house lest an important telephone call might come, but nothing of importance happened.

Miss Wilcox was invited to dinner on Thursday night for two reasons: to see the Jordons in their home, even though one member would be absent, and to give an account of the board meeting that would have been held that day. She brought no news, however. "It was postponed," she had to tell them. "The President of the board is at the shore and won't come back until Monday.

"These things always work slowly, Mrs. Jordon," she said, when she and Tippy were alone in the living room and Marny was doing the dishes with Tippy Two a willing assistant and Petey, equally willing, more of a hindrance than a help. "They take time."

"We don't have much time," Tippy replied dolefully. "I don't understand why they can't see how good it will be for Marny, and just let her go."

"Because there's so much for them to consider." Doris Wilcox began an explanation that Tippy had heard before, and it wasn't until a new sentence caught her attention that she looked startled. "There's the matter of payments," Miss Wilcox was saying, "and which state will have to make them. I'm afraid New York will refuse to take on the expense of a ward who doesn't belong to it, and Georgia will try to cancel out."

"Oh, we don't want *money* for taking care of Marny!"

Tippy cried. "If that's all that's holding everything up, tell them to forget it."

"But you will be paid, you know. Foster parents are always paid for the expense and care of a minor in their custody. It isn't a fortune," she said, smiling, "but you'll receive what the Bullocks did. It comes under the state's welfare program. A letter of inquiry was sent off to your county seat in New York today."

"Oh, murder." Tippy stared across the room at Miss Wilcox as she exclaimed, "A letter can't get all the way up to New York until tomorrow, even if you sent it air mail—perhaps not until Saturday—and nobody *works* on Saturday! And should they send an answer back on Monday, we wouldn't hear anything until too late to. . . . Oh, Miss Wilcox," she implored, "can't you just decide that Marny can go with us, then work out the money end of it later?"

"No." Miss Wilcox shook her head regretfully, and added, "that's only one snag. We have to receive the authority to transfer Marny."

"And you don't have that, yet?"

"No, but it's being worked on." It was a flat statement that made Miss Wilcox shake her head again. "We. . . ." She stopped because Marny and her helpers came in at that moment. Nothing more could be discussed.

The whole business was too complicated and slow-moving to suit Tippy. She felt so helpless without Peter to sustain her. She was sure he could find some way either through or around this dilemma, but she could only wait until Friday. And after that would come another long, useless weekend.

She was dressing for the party at the club when she heard

65

a car pull into the driveway; and with her dress half on, she ran to the window. A young sergeant in Peter's command had driven him home from the airport.

"Thanks, Herb," Peter said, getting out with his brief case. "When you come to Vietnam I'll do a favor for you."

"Just get me in your outfit, sir," Sergeant Mullholland answered with a grin.

"Will do. Thanks again, and I'll see you Monday."

Peter slammed the car door and leaped up the two steps to the kitchen just in time to collide with Tippy. "Oh, Peter," she cried, flinging her arms about his neck, "I never was so glad to see you. Did everything go all right for you?"

"Just fine. I've got some great news."

She was sure it would be about Marny, so it surprised her to hear him say, "I get a two-week R and R leave after I've been in Vietnam six months. Isn't that swell?"

"What's an R and R leave?" she asked, feeling a twinge of disappointment.

He took time to kiss her upturned face before he answered, "It's Rest and Recreation. I can go to Bangkok or Hong Kong or Australia or Hawaii."

"Why, Peter, it's wonderful!" she cried, happy for him.

"But that isn't the best of it," he went on. "We can save our pennies to fly you over to wherever I go, and we can enjoy my leave together."

"Really? You mean we'll be together again in *six months?*"

"Six months from the day I land in Saigon." He managed to lay his brief case on the counter so he could hug her properly, and as his hands met on her bare back he said,

"Turn around so I can zip you. How are you ever going to get yourself dressed for six whole months before I see you again?" he teased.

"Marny will have to do it," Tippy said, bending her head so the zipper could slide up. And she asked, "Do I bring the children with me to wherever we're going?"

"Nope. I figured that out on the plane. I love my children," he said, "but this is to be our second honeymoon. With Marny to look after them, you can park them with some of the family and they won't miss any school."

"But Marny may not be with us." The zipper was in place, and Peter had found a small hidden hook that secured it, so she turned back to him and mirrored his happy gray eyes in her sober tan ones. "From what Doris Wilcox told me," she said, "it may take forever and ever to get her."

"Hm. Things are snarled, huh?" he asked, watching her nod. And that was when he made a key remark that should have meant something to her at the time, but didn't. "I wish I knew someone in the government with a lot of rank," he said, before he hurriedly released her and braced himself to receive two small flying missiles that were heading straight at him.

Tippy and Peter went to their weekend parties. Peter returned to duty on Monday, and Tippy, leaving Marny stationed near the telephone, rushed out to shop. She brought home summer dresses for Marny to try on, returned the ones that didn't fit, and brought others. She seemed to be always in transit, and between trips she tried to locate the will-o'-the-wisp Doris Wilcox. She received no satisfactory reports from her, and on Wednesday the big moving van came.

Treasured furniture was whisked out by men who had no appreciation of its value to the Jordons. It was pushed and shoved, and finally stacked inside the van in an oblong of space that was smaller than the smallest of the seven rooms that had housed it. After the van had left, Tippy paced back and forth on the living-room carpeting that the Pattersons had bought. The empty house was so—empty.

Peter had gone for the cots. Marny, despairing but trying not to show it, had taken Tippy Two and Petey to a roadside drive-in for hamburgers and malted milks. Tippy wandered restlessly from one room to the other. Tomorrow, no matter what happened, they would have to leave Atlanta. Eighteen hours from now at the latest. Their house would be gone, and even if they could afford to wait days and days in a motel, it wouldn't be fair to Peter, who was counting on using his precious leave to see his father and brothers and sisters, and to settle his little family safely in near them.

What to do? Should they abandon Marny? Never! Tippy sat down on the floor; she got up; she wandered from window to window—and it was when she was staring at the silent, useless telephone on the bottom step of the stairway that Peter's remark caught in a groove of her brain, and tap-tapped a message. "I wish I knew someone in the government with a lot of rank," he had said. Rank? Whom did they know with political rank? Tippy sat down beside the telephone to recover from the bolt of lightning that had struck her. Any high-ranking army officer would be of no help because he had no power in a civilian government. Who then?

Congressman Corrigan, of New York? "I went all the way up there to vote for him, and he's a friend of David's," she told the telephone receiver as she snatched it up to dial long distance. "Even if he doesn't know who I am, he can tell that I'm desperate or I wouldn't bother him. He has to help me."

It took a full ten minutes for the operator to reach the Congressman's office in Washington and to inform Tippy, via a secretary, that Congress had adjourned for the summer and that Congressman Corrigan was vacationing in Canada. Would she speak with someone else?

"No, thank you," Tippy said dully, staring at the silent receiver. That slim hope was gone. Who else could she think of? Nobody. Then another thought clicked. She remembered Senator Robinson. She didn't know him, but his son was one of her nephew Davy's roommates at West Point. Davy had saved John Robinson from going absent without leave during their first year and wrecking his chance to become an army officer. If she could just talk to Davy, he would know where the Senator lived. Another call, to West Point this time, brought her the information that Davy was on his way to duty at Camp Upton, training the new cadets, and couldn't be reached by telephone before tomorrow. John Robinson, she learned, when she gave his name in desperation, had just left Fort Knox, Kentucky, for West Point.

"Thank you," Tippy said again; and before the operator could cut the connection she gave Penny's number at Round Tree Farm.

The Senator might like to do Davy a favor for saving John's career, she reasoned, and he might like to do one for Penny's daughter also. Brave, impulsive Parri, feeling sorry for John, had taken it upon herself to telephone the Senator and tell him that it was quite all right for him to marry again, but that John had run away from West Point because *somebody* had to look after his motherless little brother and sister whom the Senator seemed to have forgotten he had. Senator Robinson had been grateful to Parri for the deserved scolding she audaciously gave him and had promptly brought his children from Kansas to Washington, where his fiancée had accepted them and learned to love them. The whole MacDonald family had been invited to the wedding.

"Hello?" she heard her sister Penny say, and at Tippy's quavering reply, she cried, "Is that you, Tip? Are you on your way up here?"

"Not till tomorrow," Tippy said, hurrying on. "I haven't time to talk to you now because I have to speak to Parri."

"She isn't here," Penny answered. "She went to a picnic, but won't I do as well?"

"I don't think so, but—well, maybe you can help me." Tippy launched briefly into her dilemma. "I just have until tomorrow," she ended. "I can't explain things very well, but Mums knows all about it."

"I do, too," Penny said, "via the family grapevine. Do you want Parri to call Senator Robinson when she comes home?"

"It would be too late," Tippy answered, sighing, her last hope gone.

"Then wait a minute. I have his address somewhere. We sent a wedding gift to his wife's place in Virginia, and I wrote it down in an old notebook. Hold on."

From the way her voice faded, Tippy knew she had the telephone cradled in her shoulder and was looking through a desk drawer. "You could call him now and explain that you're Parri's aunt," she said above the rattle of paper.

70

"Oh, here it is. If he should be out in Kansas or whatever state he represents, someone at this number can tell you where to find him. Be sure to tell him that you're Parri's aunt," she reminded, "Parri's and Davy's. Have you a pencil and paper?"

Tippy didn't need to write down the number; it would be etched in her brain. "Yes," she said, closing her eyes while she repeated the digits Penny gave her. "Thanks, Pen, I'll see you Sunday evening." And she broke the connection.

Down went the receiver again, and in her rush she forgot to wait for the dial tone. After she had struggled with three operators, hers, Virginia's, and Information, a woman's pleasant voice answered the ringing telephone. "Hello," it said, and Tippy started all over again.

"Is Senator Robinson there?" she asked. "This is Andrea Jordon calling from Atlanta, Georgia, and I would like very much to speak with him."

"Oh, I'm sorry, but he isn't here," the voice returned, sounding genuinely regretful. "He just drove into town to the hardware store on an errand for me. I'm Mrs. Robinson, and is there anything I can do for you?"

"I don't know. Perhaps. . . ." Tippy repeated her well-remembered lines. She gave a longer explanation of her difficulty than she had wasted on Penny because the voice at the other end of the line kept asking interested questions.

"I do understand your predicament," it said, making Tippy like it even more than she had at first. "It's a fine thing you're doing, and I know Bill will think so, too. I do wish he were here. Where did you say you live?"

"Not anywhere, right now," Tippy answered. "The girl

we're trying to help, Marian Alexander, lives here in Atlanta, but we're leaving tomorrow. I was so desperate to find Senator Robinson that I tried to call Davy, then John, for his address. Parri's mother gave it to me."

"Oh, you're Davy's aunt, and Parri's too!" the voice exclaimed. "Now I know who you are. I do wish Bill were here, but I can give him your message just as soon as he comes home. He only went to a couple of stores so he won't be long. Suppose I do that and have him call you back?"

"Oh, *would* you do that?" Tippy thought her voice screeched like a child's pleading for a piece of candy, but she couldn't control it. "I'd be so appreciative of any advice from Senator Robinson. If he could just tell us what to do and whom to see, we would be so grateful."

"I'm sure he'll want to do what he can," Mrs. Robinson promised. "We never can repay Davy and Parri for all they did for us. We're a happy family now, thanks to them. I'll watch for Bill, and he'll be in touch with you very soon."

"Thank you. Good-by." Tippy laid down the receiver with the feeling that help was on the way.

She was still sitting beside the telephone, waiting for the return call, when Marny came in. "Has anything happened, Aunt Tippy?" she whispered, so the trailing Tippy Two and Petey couldn't hear.

They were coaxing Switzy in from the garage where he had taken refuge when the movers arrived, and listening to them shout into his deafness that he would be starting off on a long, hot trip tomorrow, Tippy said brightly, "Not yet, but it will. You're going with us, Marny, even if I have to kidnap you. I'm waiting now for a very important call."

She waited all afternoon. Peter came home with the cots, and while he set them up in the different bedrooms she told him what she had done. "Mrs. Robinson assured me that the Senator would call me right back," she said disconsolately, while she tore up a discarded bedspread to cover five hard pillows for which she had no cases. "He hasn't, and it's been two whole hours. Do you think she forgot to tell him?"

"I doubt it, not if she was as interested as you say she sounded. Not after you mentioned John and Parri and Davy."

"I was so happy for a while," Tippy said, sitting down on one of the cots and looking up at him. "I was so proud of you for telling me what to do."

"I told you?" Peter straightened from unfolding a cot and turned to stare at her. "Why, I didn't tell you to call the Senator, Tip."

"No, but you told me that we needed to find someone with rank, so I did. I never would have thought of it by myself, and now it's too late to do anything he might suggest. All the offices will be closed."

"We still have tomorrow, Tippy," he tried to comfort her. "We don't have to leave until we get this impasse worked out, and we can even stay on a few days if we have to. Your father said he'd see that the furniture gets put in storage."

But she only laid a pillow on her own sheet-draped cot and said, "I suppose I'd better go down and see what Marny and the children are doing."

Marny, not knowing what else to do, had sat down on one of the chairs of the breakfast set that the Pattersons had bought. Tippy Two and Petey had taken Switzy for a farewell call on the Johnstons next door, and she was alone.

What is to become of me? she thought wretchedly, staring out at the empty back yard. Aunt Tippy can't kidnap me. I know that. The police would only catch up with us and bring me back. And what will they do with me after the Jordons have to go off and leave me? Will the Bullocks take me back? I don't think so, because they don't really want me.

Her winter clothes were traveling northward on a van; her portable typewriter was in one of the big trunks that had been sent by express; and only five new dresses and four old ones that had been shortened hung in her closet. Marny sighed as she remembered her joy when she had tried on the new dresses and her relief when her Aunt Tippy had said, "We can afford them, Marny, because you are going to be a young lady of means now," and had explained about the monthly check they would receive.

The dresses would have to be returned to the store, Marny knew, and the yellow coat that had been reduced, and the white sweater, and the two pairs of shorts. She couldn't pay back all the money her Aunt Tippy had spent. Whoever took her now would expect to keep the monthly check. What would she do? Where would she go? Her heart pounded so hard with fear that she couldn't think. She tried to tell herself that she had been given ten unexpected days of happiness, at least, and that the Jordons loved her and would find some way to send for her later, so she mustn't let whatever happened to her in the meantime matter. She couldn't do it. Her present disappointment and loss were too great. She could only put her head down on the table and quietly cry.

"Why, darling, you mustn't give up!" Tippy exclaimed, coming out to the kitchen and finding her huddled there. "We won't go off and leave you. I promised you that."

Then she pulled another chair closer and sat down to take the shaking little figure in her arms. "A few days in a motel," she said, "and everything will be straightened out. I know it will."

"I can't let you waste Uncle Major's leave," Marny sobbed against her. "I've already caused you so much trouble and expense."

"Oh, pooh." Tippy smoothed back Marny's brown hair and smiled at her as she said, "We want you, darling. We want you to live with us. We want to help you. And we will try every way to do it. You must believe it's possible. Say over and over to yourself, 'Nothing can keep me from living with Aunt Tippy and Uncle Major. Nothing, nothing, nothing.' "

"I'll try to." Marny made an effort to answer Tippy's confident smile with a feeble one, but tears gathered in her eyes again, as she said, "Aunt Tippy, nobody in the whole world is as good as you and Uncle Major. I do want to go with you, but even if I can't, I can always love you. The whole wonderful part of it is that I have someone to love."

"And a family to love you," Tipply replied softly, kissing Marny's wet cheek. Then she stood up to say resolutely, "We must believe that you're going. Let's declare it together while we get dinner."

They made sloppy Joes in the one big pan they had saved out; and while Marny set the table with paper plates and plastic forks and spoons, they turned the words into a rhyme that they sang together: "Marny is going with us, hooray, hooray. Marny is going with us, today, today. We'll all start out in our poor old car, and we won't care how hot we are, because Marny is going with us. Hooray, hooray."

Peter came in while they were laughing and improving their hit album, added a couple of lines of his own, and the children returned to shout the "hoorays." Switzy, hearing nothing but sensing the merriment, added his excited bark.

Sloppy Joes, sliced tomatoes, and the last half of a watermelon were eaten around the table with everyone being gay and a little silly. But when the meal was over, when the kitchen was spotless again, when Marny had taken Tippy Two and Peter out for a last splash in the pool that was to be left as a parting gift to the Pattersons, when Peter had gone upstairs to finish his packing, Tippy went into the living room to sit down on the floor and stare at the telephone. Senator Robinson had let her down, in spite of the great interest his wife had shown in the Jordons' plight. Perhaps she had forgotten to tell him, or, more likely, perhaps he hadn't cared enough to call back.

That isn't the way Davy helped his son, Tippy thought resentfully. He risked his whole future as a cadet to rush to a hotel that was off limits and hustle John back before he would be missed. She considered calling Miss Wilcox again or Mr. Bosserman, but was sure it would be useless. They would have called her long before this had any decision been made. Nothing more could be done until tomorrow, if anything could be done at all. Then, at eight o'clock, the telephone rang.

She sprang up and crossed the floor in three leaps. Jerking it from the newel post where it now rested, she flopped down on the bottom step of the stairway and clapped the receiver to her ear. "Yes? Hello?" she said breathlessly, expecting to hear Doris Wilcox answer her. But a deep rumbling voice came back.

"Mrs. Jordon?" it asked; and at her nod that couldn't be heard, it said, "This is Senator Robinson. I'm sorry to get back to you so late but I've been rather busy."

"Oh, I'm sure you have," Tippy murmured politely, assuming that the Senator had been happily pounding in nails from the hardware store.

But he went on, "It has taken me until now to track down that Governor of yours. He had just come home to dinner when I caught him." There was a pleased chuckle, then Senator Robinson said, "Your troubles are over."

"They—are?" Tippy's heart got in the way of her voice. She couldn't speak around it. She could only listen to Peter, who had come in on the upstairs extension.

"This is Peter Jordon, Senator," he said. "My wife, who is downstairs, seems to be in a state of joyous collapse."

"Then I'll talk to you," Senator Robinson said, sounding more official than he had with Tippy. "The Governor appreciates the fine thing you two are doing and will give the order for your young ward to leave Atlanta with you tomorrow. Naturally, there will be a few details left unsettled," the Senator explained. "An agreement between Georgia and New York must be reached. Since I understand that you will be leaving quite soon for Vietnam, Mrs. Jordon may have to return to Atlanta at a later date."

"She can do that," Peter said, knowing that Tippy would get back some way. "Do we pick up a legal paper before we leave?"

"Yes." There was a pause while the Senator consulted his notes for names he wanted; then he said, "Mr. Bosserman of the State and County Welfare Department will have been advised by now that he is to release Marian Alexander into your custody. He will be ready for you whenever you drop by."

"Thank you, sir. We can't tell you how grateful we are." Peter would have said more, but to his surprise Tippy's voice wavered in again.

"How did you ever manage it, Senator?" she asked, eager and breathless.

"Oh, it was easy," the Senator replied. "I know the Governor quite well, and by the way, Major," he said, speaking to Peter again, "I hope you will give my regards to your father."

"Do you know Dad?" Peter asked.

"Yes, but he doesn't know me." There was another chuckling pause before Senator Robinson said, "I was his relief driver on Guam for four days when his regular driver was out with a virus. I hope he won't remember that the staff car blew a tire on my very first day and made him late for a meeting. I was sure I was going to lose my sergeant's stripes but the General was swell about it. You know," he said conversationally, as Peter was about to assure him that his father never remembered inconveniences, "the Jordon family is tops with me."

"Thank you, sir," Peter had only time to say before Tippy screeched in again with:

"Oh, Senator Robinson, we're the most thankful people in the whole world tonight. Marny and I will bake cakes and cookies to take up to John, and we'll have him and

Davy over whenever they have a free day. Oh, *thank* you, Senator Robinson."

"No thanks needed. If you give my boy a little extra kindness, that is all the thanks I ask—and from what I know of you, you're quite free with kindness."

She could hear Peter saying last good-bys from upstairs, but she sat with the receiver dangling between her knees. She was too spent to speak. She was like a track contestant in a meet who had run and run and run, then given a last gasping sprint to break the tape.

Peter came leaping down the stairway. He took the receiver from her nerveless hand, replaced the telephone on the newel post, then pulled her up into his arms. "It's all over, Tippy," he comforted, to stop her trembling. "Marny's going. She's going, hooray, hooray!"

"I know it." Tippy frowned at him and said the last thing he expected to hear. "Marny needs a permanent," she wailed. "We've been planning to give her one but we haven't had time."

He had been sure, knowing Tippy, that she would go tearing out to find Marny, shrieking the news as she ran, and here she stood, stewing about Marny's hair.

"Take her to your beauty shop tomorrow and let them fix her up," he suggested, trying not to laugh. "I'll have to sign out, and if we don't get off until four or five o'clock, it won't matter."

"I guess I can." His wilted blossom suddenly stiffened like a flower that had been fed an aspirin tablet. "Oh, goodness!" she cried. "What are we doing in *here?* We should be telling Marny!" And together they raced out to the wading pool.

5

Marny lay on her hard army cot that felt as soft to her as frothy soap bubbles. She was going, her heart sang. She was *definitely* going. The words Tippy had told her to repeat with assurance could now be said with joy. At some unspecified hour tomorrow, Marny Alexander could walk out of the house with the Jordons and take her place on the back seat of the car.

"Oh, thank You, God," she whispered, as she had at intervals ever since she came up to her room. And she added with great determination, "I really must go to sleep now."

She knew she must because tomorrow was to be such a busy, glorious day. But how could she when such happy thoughts kept buzzing through her head? She wanted to get up and pad across the bare floor to look at the new dresses that were packed in a big suitcase that matched the one Tippy Two had. Were they folded so they wouldn't wrinkle? Had she put in the two pairs of new shorts with their sleeveless blouses? Had she given her yellow coat to Aunt Tippy to put in the hanger case with the other coats? She thought she had, just as she was almost sure that everything she would need on the trip was in the one case she and the children would share in the motels where they were to stop. Her blue-and-white-checked dress was in there, and her new candy-striped drip-dry was hanging in the closet, ready to put on tomorrow when she discarded her old blue shorts and shirt. There was no need to look at everything again she decided, trying to turn over in her narrow space without making a clatter on the bare floor.

"Now go to sleep," she ordered herself sternly. "Remember what Grandma used to tell you about Christmas morning. 'It will come a lot sooner if you sleep the night away.'" And she clamped her eyelids shut.

Morning did come in a rush for everyone. Breakfast, such as it was, was eaten on paper plates; orange juice was drunk from paper cups; and anyone who wanted cereal had it in a chipped bowl that was rinsed out for the next one. Marny was whisked off for her long-awaited permanent. Peter and Tippy took the children with them while Peter signed out from his tour of duty in Atlanta, and they picked up Marny's valuable paper that would declare her to be no longer under the jurisdiction of the State of Georgia.

"Oh, you do look darling," Tippy cried, when they came back to the beauty shop and she saw the new Marny. "Jean cut it just right. Shorter around your face and curling around your cheeks, then dipping down longer in the back. I knew she would. Why, Marny, you're so *pretty!*"

"Oh, Aunt Tippy!" Marny blushed with pleasure because she knew there was some truth in Tippy's words. She had watched in the mirror while the operator arranged her hair, brushing a soft bang to one side. "I'm sure I can keep it like this," she said happily, when they went out to the car to be met by a trio of compliments. And she bent her head to ask anxiously, "Jean didn't get the collar of my dress wrinkled, did she?"

"Nary a wrinkle," Tippy assured her, smoothing the collar and adding a pat. "Now, let's hurry," she said to Peter as she slid in beside him. "We might eat lunch at The Barbecue Pit so we can get off early."

The telephone was ringing when they reached their immaculate, empty house. It rang constantly, because the Pattersons would take it over after today and would send all previous charges to the Jordons in New York. Miss Wilcox called to say she would be coming out to tell them a quick good-by.

Tippy hoped to have a few uninterrupted, grateful moments with her, but friends poured in. They hampered Peter's loading of the car. They shoved rolled raincoats, the sheets, a bag of soiled laundry into spots that Peter was saving, and they put the overnight cases where he couldn't possibly reach them without tearing the whole luggage compartment apart.

"Don't worry about it, Tip," he said, when he was left holding her bottle case that would have to ride between her feet. "I'll repack everything tonight when we stop. Just get Switzy in and park him."

Switzy was nervous in all the confusion. He couldn't hear

what was being said, but from having lived with the Jordons all his life, he knew he was on the move again. Rollo had always been with him before. Rollo, his ears as sensitive as a microphone, had been accustomed to moving from here to there in the army. He had taken it in his short-legged stride and had always told Switzy what to expect. There was no Rollo now, so Switzy waited patiently until he was put in the middle of the front seat. It was not his accustomed place. He and Rollo had always ridden in back with one of the children beside them, but he lay down where Tippy plopped him and put his nose between his paws.

"Are the Thermos bottles and the box of cookies in?" she asked, ticking off important necessities on her fingers.

"Yep." Tippy Two pointed to the ledge below the rear window.

"Do the Pattersons have the keys?"

"Yep." Peter's voice answered her.

"Switzy's water bowl?" Marny had it. "The camera? Oh, I put it in the glove compartment myself." She leaned across Switzy to make sure, then backed out into the group of spectators that stood like a chorus waiting for the principals to leave the stage. "Well, I guess we're ready to go," she said, beginning her round of good-byes.

She saved Miss Wilcox until last because she saw her talking earnestly with Marny. The children were in the car. Peter, halfway in, was calling, "Come on, Tip," so she could only take both of Doris Wilcox's hands in hers, and, holding them tightly, say, "You'll never know how grateful we are. Marny and I are going to be awfully lonely after Peter leaves, so please try to come up to visit us."

"I will, and I'll keep in touch with you," Miss Wilcox

promised, as Tippy gave her a hasty kiss and went rushing off.

She slid in, closed the door, and scooped up Switzy to put him on her lap and let him look out. She heard Petey complain, "I want to sit by a window like Tippy Two is," then turned around to watch Marny squeeze him past her knees and take the middle seat herself. There were calls of "Good-by," "Drive carefully," "Write to us," while arms waved from both outside and inside the car's open windows; Switzy gave sharp, excited barks, and the car began to move along the driveway into the street.

"Oh, golly, I can't believe it," Tippy said, looking over Switzy's head for a last glimpse of her house. "We're on our way and it isn't quite three o'clock. We're starting on the very day we planned to and all of us are here. One, two, three, four, five, six," she counted happily, ruffling Switzy's topknot. "Oh, Peter, I didn't have time to feel sorry about leaving Atlanta."

"That's good." Peter thought it was more than that; it was a miracle. Tippy, like a contented cat, never wanted to leave her familiar surroundings. And to prevent nostalgia from attacking her at this late hour, he handed her a map of Georgia that he had marked, and said, "Get on the job, girl. Tell me when to take the Y that will put us on the super-duper highway."

The whole trip northward was a dream trip to Marny. She had never stayed in a luxurious motel, had never eaten in a big dining room. The longest motor trip she had ever taken was when she had gone with Mrs. Bullock to visit a sick friend who lived sixty miles away. This was all new and exciting to her. At six o'clock she followed the family into two beautifully furnished bedrooms, watched a rollaway bed appear for Petey as if by magic, opened the small suitcase Peter set on the luggage rack, unpacked the night clothes they would need, saw that her lively little roommates were showered and dressed, and found time to brush her beautiful new hair-do.

She was clinging numbly to Tippy Two's hand when they entered the dining room and were shown to a table for five. A large menu enclosed in a black-and-gold cardboard cover was laid before her on the white tablecloth, and she glanced quickly about to watch the others open the ones they had. Tippy Two studied hers as if accustomed to doing it, but Petey immediately announced, "I want steak."

"You'll have your choice of meats on the children's dinner," his mother informed him, winking at his father. "You can have fried chicken, salisbury steak, or liver. Take your choice."

"Chicken," he said; and Tippy Two seconded the order.

Marny looked down the printed menu until she found the children's dinner at the very bottom of the page. It was expensive. Even the simplest entree cost more than she could earn in a whole day of baby sitting. "Aunt Tippy," she said, her eyes just showing above the big folder, "I'm not very hungry. Could I have a cup of soup, please?"

"Nonsense, sugar." Tippy reached across Petey to take the menu from Marny. "Why don't you have what I'm going to order?" she suggested. "Veal scallopini. I've had it in the Holiday Inns before, and it's always delicious." Then she leaned even closer to say, "We're going to live it up for two nights, or possibly three, since we got a late start: Uncle Major wants us to."

"All right, if you think I should." Marny looked inquiringly at Peter, who grinned and nodded.

So she learned to eat and sleep in motels. She was the happiest, cheeriest one on the trip. She colored with Tippy Two, drilled toy soldiers with Petey, exclaimed with delight over the changes in scenic beauty, and took Switzy for his evening and early-morning walk. And when they left the New Jersey Turnpike for the Garden State Parkway that bypassed New York City, she stared at the skyline in the distance with breathless awe and wonder.

"We're almost there," she heard her Aunt Tippy say with a sigh of relief, late Sunday afternoon. "We made good time today, Peter."

Marny could have gone on and on forever, just as they were, safely enclosed in the car. There would be strangers to meet, people who were her Aunt Tippy's and Uncle Peter's parents and brothers and sisters and nieces and nephews. She knew how they would look from having studied the photographs that had been arranged on the long bookshelves in silver frames. She was sure she could unerringly recognize each one. But could she speak to them, calling him or her by name? Could she be brave enough to say, "Aunt Carrol," "Uncle David," and on down the line as Aunt Tippy wanted her to do? And what should she call Colonel and Mrs. Parrish and General Jordon? She supposed she would have to do as she had done with Uncle Major at first, look directly at them whenever she needed to speak to them.

Oh, dear, she groaned inwardly, when they stopped on the outskirts of a town, at a motel that was smaller than the ones she had grown accustomed to. I'm so nervous. I'm exactly where I want to be but I'm scared. What if nobody likes me and wonders why Aunt Tippy wanted to bring me with her?

"All out," Peter said, cutting into her dismal thoughts, and opening the back door of the car while Tippy went racing into the motel's lobby and a telephone. "Showers are in order and a quick change; then we head for the family gathering."

Marny was relieved when her best dress came out of the big suitcase unwrinkled. She had spread tissue paper between its soft yellow gores, and when she shook it out it looked as well-pressed as it had when she packed it. Tippy Two hustled into her white dress, and Petey into his white shirt and shorts, on crooked as usual, because he was in a great hurry to go to his Aunt Carrol's and Uncle David's. Marny fumbled and procrastinated. She even tried to delay her ordeal by suggesting that she take Switzy for a walk. But that was vetoed.

"Why, he has a whole park to run in at Gladstone," Tippy Two said, as if Marny should know it. "Come on. Mums and Daddy are waiting for us."

Later, much later, Marny wondered why she had been reluctant to meet the rest of this affectionate family. They had driven between enormous gateposts, wound along for a quarter of a mile through the parkland that Tippy Two had spoken about, before they swung into a circular driveway that had flowers and a fountain in the middle of it. Marny had stared and stared at the sight of Gladstone rising against the skyline. It was higher and longer than any of the motels she had stayed in. It was like the castles she had seen in movies. She couldn't believe that any one family could live in a house this big.

"Perkins will come out to receive us," her Aunt Tippy

turned her head to say into her wide-eyed staring. "He's the old butler Carrol has had ever since she was a little girl. He's an old dear, so don't let him throw you."

"Should I shake hands with him?" Marny managed to ask, and Tippy nodded.

"You're family," she said, "and he'd like that. I have a special pat I always give him, and Petey almost knocks him down when he hugs him around the knees. Yes, shake hands with him."

Marny remembered that, but it was hard to do. Perkins opened the great oak doors but was lost in the crowd that came pouring out. The dusty car was besieged like an Apache attack on a fort. There were welcoming hugs and kisses, and in the midst of them, Marny found herself clasped in loving embraces.

"Darlings, we're so glad you're here at last," the beautiful blond hostess, who must be Carrol Parrish, said. "David has been walking around with his eyes on his watch, and Davy was simply sunk because he had to go back to the Academy before you came. John Robinson telephoned to know if you have Marny and—where is Marny?" she paused to ask. "I'm sure I saw her but where is she?"

"Right here with me." Tippy pulled Marny up the broad steps and managed to hold on to her even though she had one arm around her mother. "This is our Marny," she said proudly. "Marny, this is your Aunt Carrol and your Grandmother Parrish." Then she looked back at the group still surrounding the car, and asked, "Where's Daddy Jordon?"

"He and Miss Bitsy got held up in New York, Miss Tippy," Perkins informed her, holding open one of the massive doors; and that was when Marny was able to give the very British butler her shy handshake.

So many Parrishes, so many Jordons. An impressive drawing room like the ones Marny had seen in movies was filled with them. They moved about so rapidly that she had difficulty in sorting them out.

"Hello, there," one of the new uncles said, coming over to the yellow brocade sofa where she had discreetly taken refuge; and looking up at him she knew he had to be Bobby Parrish. He looked like both Colonel Parrish and his son David, but he had the merriest blue eyes she had ever seen.

"I'm glad Tippy brought us a pretty niece," he went on. "All of them—except my child, of course—are so homely. That one is mine." He pointed proudly to a small girl who was being led off to bed by a pretty mother who bore a slight resemblance to Marny's Uncle Major, in that she was tall and had the same wheat-colored hair, and said with fatherly pride, "She's a doll."

"Parri is pretty, too," Marny replied, watching a sparkling brown-eyed girl who, coming toward her, had stopped to say something to a woman who could only be the famous actress Penny Parrish, and Parrish MacDonald's mother.

"Hi, Marny," Parri said, a little loftily, because, after all, being almost seventeen makes one much older than someone who is only fifteen. "Have you got us all straightened out, yet?"

"Not quite," Marny answered thinking a dark, teen-aged boy might be Parri's brother because he looked like the craggy man who had just linked arms with her mother.

"Well, I'll see if I can help you." Parri said a pert, "Good by, Uncle Bobby," and sat down on the sofa beside Marny. "That's Grandpa talking with Aunt Tippy and Uncle

Peter, and that's Lang over there, teasing Carli. He's Aunt Carrol's and Uncle David's second son, and he goes to college. Carli is theirs too, and she's eleven or maybe twelve —I never can remember." They sat talking together, with Parri adding footnotes about each one she pointed out, and she had made very little progress when Perkins announced dinner.

The dining room presented another surprise to Marny. She had never seen a dining room, except in The Home, that could hold such a long table. This one was covered by a white linen-and-lace cloth topped by four candelabra, and seventeen people were finding places along it, with two chairs still left vacant. Marny supposed they were for General Jordon and the aunt whom she hadn't yet met.

She was relieved to find that she was seated between Parri and the uncle with the twinkling eyes. "I showed you which one Lang is, didn't I?" Parri asked, grinning across the table at a cousin whose haughty profile was made to look even haughtier by a thin, high-bridged nose. "Mr. Langdon Houghton Parrish. He's named for his other grandfather and he looks just like him. He says he's planning to make even more money than his grandpappy did."

"Oh, shut up. I heard you," Lang retorted, scowling across the table at her. But Parri only grinned and tossed her head.

"Eavesdroppers never hear any good about themselves," she retorted, letting her finger move on to a pretty little blond girl who was helping Petey scoop up a melon ball that had popped out of its long-stemmed glass. "I pointed Carli out to you, too, and she's a darling. She looks and acts so much like Aunt Carrol. Now, let me see," she said, looking around Marny for any cousin whom she might have missed. "There's Joshu. He's my brother and he's thirteen. He used to be an awful drag but he's improved a lot. I'm growing very fond of him," Parri admitted. "And after Mums and Dad go off to Hollywood. . . ." She broke off to ask, "You know they're going out there so Mums can make a picture, don't you?" And at Marny's nod, she went on, "I think Joshu and I will be very compatible. That's Mums down there by Aunt Tippy."

Marny knew which member of the family was Penny Parrish MacDonald. Having once seen her, it was impossible to forget her. She shone like Venus in a sky full of bright stars. I don't think I'd be afraid to talk to her, Marny thought in her private cataloguing. She's as natural as Aunt Tippy is, or Uncle David or even Uncle Bobby.

Her eyes turned to study Bobby Parrish, who was talking seriously across the table, and he broke off his conversation to say to her, "I've watched you giving us all a good once-over, and you look like a pretty astute little character to me. Do we shape up like you thought we would?"

Marny was saved an embarrassed reply because the double doors were thrown open and General Jordon came in. He looked like his photograph: big, ruddy, with iron-gray hair and a clipped mustache.

"Glad we didn't hold you up," he said to both Carrol and David at opposite ends of the table. Then he kissed Tippy and shook Peter's hand.

He looked austere to Marny, but her Aunt Tippy had said he wasn't. She said he cleared his throat and made hurrumphing noises from shyness. It must be true, Marny thought, because he came along the table with Tippy Two and Petey hanging on him. "Now, run back to your chairs and sit down," he said to them in a gruff way that failed to dislodge them. "I want to meet our new girl. Where is she?" he asked.

Marny stood up. "I'm here, sir," she said around a maid who was exchanging the first course for a dinner plate. "I'm Marny."

"I'm delighted to know you, Marny. We've—hur-rumph —heard a lot about you, and we'll get acquainted later."

"Thank you, sir." Marny was about to sit down again when a pretty girl with pale swinging hair came in.

"Oh, I'm sorry we're late and disrupting things," she apologized to the table in general. Then she kissed both Tippy and Peter; and with Tippy Two and Petey transferring themselves from their grandfather to her like a couple of plasters, she came around the table to give Marny a hug. "I'm your new Aunt Bitsy," she said, having been well briefed beforehand. "You can call me Bitsy as the other kids do. I never have felt very auntish." Then she laughed and said, "Please sit down everybody. It's all Daddy's fault that we're late, and I'm even later. He would drive in town in Sunday traffic to pick me up, and he would come in that convertible of his that always leaves me looking like a windblown mess. I had to stop and comb my hair. Oh, thanks, Peter."

Peter was holding a chair for her, and as she slid quickly into it, she said, "Daddy and I will skip whatever courses you've had and catch up with you."

It was a short but fabulous evening to Marny. She could call them all by name now, with the exception of Colonel and Mrs. Parrish and General Jordon. She could answer those three only when they spoke directly to her. They weren't her grandparents and she couldn't call them uncle or aunt because she didn't know their first names. I'll ask Aunt Tippy what I should do, she decided, when everyone was saying good-by and making plans for tomorrow.

This whole wonderful family had welcomed her. All of them had accepted her just as if she truly belonged to them.

"Oh, Aunt Tippy," she said almost tearfully, when they were back in the car with Petey leaning against her, sound asleep, "I think I'm the happiest girl in the whole world tonight. Everybody was so—so kind and loving to me."

"That's because you're such a darling," Tippy answered, moving Switzy's head from her lap so she could twist around to send a smile back into the dimness behind her. "That's exactly why we brought you with us, isn't it, Peter?"

"Yep," he said. "You can correct me if I sound prejudiced, but I thought our three kids were the best-looking ones there."

"Oh, Uncle Major." Marny gave a soft little giggle before she said proudly, "I did look nice. My dress was every bit as pretty as Parri's. I've never had such a pretty dress before."

"And your hair looked a whole lot better than hers," Tippy commented dryly. "I don't see why Pen lets her have that brown stubble all over her head. It may be stylish but it isn't becoming to Parri."

"But she's awfully cute anyway," Marny said, wishing she had some of Parri's sparkle, just a little of it, just enough to make her seem less shy and quiet. "She told me tonight that she's going to become as good an actress as her mother is. She's already made a start. Did you know," she asked eagerly, "that she spent a whole summer in a professional theater group? When she wasn't any older than I am?"

"We all knew it," Tippy said, laughing. "She kept her parents in a constant turmoil, and they were thankful when the season ended. She's quite a girl, our Parri. I'm glad, sugar, that you don't want to be an actress."

"Oh, I don't," Marny assured her. "I don't want to do anything but live with you and Uncle Major, just go to school and come home. I can't think of anything more wonderful than that."

There was a silence for a few seconds before she said with a blissful sigh, "It's a beautiful miracle that you're giving me the chance to do it." Tippy Two's sleepy head banged against the back of the seat, and reaching out with her free hand she guided it to rest on her shoulder.

6

Marny was sitting on a wooden settee outside the motel the next morning, mending a plastic airplane for Petey and watching Tippy Two play a sort of hopscotch on the flagstoned walk, when a low-slung foreign car, its top down, came swishing to a stop before her.

"Hi," Parri MacDonald called from behind the wheel. "Come on."

Tippy Two and Petey raced out to hang on the side of the car, and Marny, after laying down the airplane, followed them. "Hop in," Parri ordered, opening the door. "I'm taking you over to my house."

"Oh, hi." Marny held Petey back as Tippy Two scrambled in behind Parri's bucket seat. "Aunt Tippy and Uncle

Major have gone with Aunt Susan to look at some houses an agent has to show them," she told Parri uncertainly. "They told us to wait here until Aunt Carrol comes to take us to Gladstone."

"My goodness, plans can change in this family in two minutes," Parri said. "Aunt Carrol heard of another house that's for rent, so she went tootling off to ask about it, and you're to come home with me."

Marny didn't know what to do. Parri was the wrong member of the family to come for them, but she looked so sure of herself, and she was urging, "Get in. You can ask Mums about it if you don't believe me."

There was nothing to do but go with her. Marny boosted Petey in, then went around the car to slide into another bucket seat beside Parri. "I didn't mean to doubt you," she apologized, watching Parri shift a gearstick that sent them off. "It's just that when Aunt Tippy tells me to do something I'm careful to do what she says."

"Oh, that's okay. You haven't lived with us long enough to know how we operate," Parri returned, shrugging. "There have been half-a-dozen calls back and forth this morning. First you were going to Aunt Carrol's, then you were going to Grandma's, then you were going to Aunt Susan's, because she didn't know what to do with Ti Me. Now Grandma has Ti Me and you're coming with us. Get it?"

Marny didn't, but she nodded. Plans never changed in the places where she had lived before. The matron of The Home held to a schedule, as did Mrs. Bullock, and she had always gone where the person in authority had told her to go. This setting out with Parri was a novel but worrisome experience. What would her Aunt Tippy say to such irresponsible behavior? "Are you sure your mother expects us?" she asked.

"I told you she does. She's always getting into everybody else's act," Parri said. "She's such a family gal that she fixed it so everybody will have to come back to our house to retrieve you and the kids. That way, she'll be in on the discussion about which house you're going to rent. Poor Mums, she hates having to go to Hollywood," Parri added sadly, as she skirted the business section of Highland Falls.

"She does?" Marny, while sitting in the beauty shop and waiting for the permanent to perform its magic, had avidly read an article in a movie magazine entitled "The Fabulous Penny Parrish." "I should think she would be thrilled," she said.

"Not Mums. She'd rather stay home and help Minna and John run the house. They're the couple who have worked for us ever since I was little. I'm slated to take Mums' place this fall," Parri went on, not mentioning that she had been such a reluctant candidate that Davy had called her "a spoiled brat" and had shamed her into accepting the responsibility. She planned to prove to Davy that she could do it. "Mums and Daddy were going in October," she said, "but Daddy got the date shoved up so they won't miss being home for Christmas, and now they're going next week, right after Joshu and I start school. I suppose you're looking forward to going to school here," she said pleasantly, sounding adult and almost like a teacher.

"Yes." Marny nodded. She could do no more than that because Parri, even with her cropped hair and faded, badly ironed green shorts, was so much older.

"I guess you'll like it," Parri said loftily. "There should be some nice kids in your class. What are you, a sophomore?"

"I'll be a junior," Marny replied, turning to hold onto Petey, who shouldn't be standing up in an open car. "I'll be sixteen in a couple of weeks," she said, giving Petey a gentle shove that put him back in the seat beside Tippy Two.

Parri concentrated on the country road ahead of her. It was narrow and curving and she had been driving for less than a month. Only the offer of this rakish car instead of the station wagon that was hers to use in a limited way had made her willing to pick up the two children and a girl who was only a couple of years older than Joshu. Now this quiet, big-eyed little thing beside her had said she would be a junior. That posed a problem.

Just this morning her mother had said, "I want you to be especially nice to Marny. She's a dear girl, and you must see that she meets an attractive crowd at school." That was when she had decided to send Parri to the motel instead of going herself.

"Do you mean I have to take her *around* with me?" Parri had screeched in agony.

"No," Penny had answered patiently. "I simply meant, since school starts next week and she won't have the opportunity to meet any girls by then, you might invite a few out here."

"Oh, all right." Parri had been resigned to giving up one afternoon. Three of her friends had younger sisters, and two had younger brothers. "I guess I could dig up some," she had agreed. "What day do you want 'em?"

"Any day that's convenient," was the answer she received. So she had started off, reluctantly resolved to do her duty.

And look what had happened. Marny would be a junior. Karen Allerdyce in her own special crowd was a junior. Karen, however, was seventeen and, through no fault of her own, had lost a year when her parents had taken the whole family off to live in some small country in Africa.

"That white house over there on your left is where Grandma and Grandpa live," she said, pulling herself out of her gloomy thoughts about the future and returning to her role of reliable guide on a tour.

"Oh." Marny had a brief glimpse of a white house set in a tree-shaded lawn, and of a man standing near a fence, waving to them. Petey had bounced to his feet again and was screaming, "Hi, Grandpa, hi, Grandpa," and she had to grab him before he pitched out of the car. "It's a pretty house," she said, seeing what she could of it around Petey. Then Parri turned a sharp corner in the road, and the house disappeared.

"I want to get out at Grandpa and Grandma's," Tippy Two rose up to say, but Parri kept on going.

"Perhaps we can come back later," Marny comforted. She was on her knees now and talking earnestly over the back of the seat to the disappointed two behind her when Parri made another right-angled turn and swished into a driveway beside a long, rambling farmhouse. When they stopped at a large screened porch, Marny wasn't sure where she was.

"Good morning, darlings!" Parri's mother cried, flinging open the door and running down the steps to them. "We're so glad you've come to spend the day with us."

She would have helped Petey out but he went with a bounce that landed him against her in a greeting that only Joshu's Saint Bernard could match.

"Where's John?" he asked, when they had righted themselves. "I want to help John run the tractor."

"He's pulling up beets in the garden and I'm sure he'll be happy to have your help," Penny answered, "so scoot." And she told Tippy Two, "Minna's baking cookies and is waiting for you to come in and spoon the batter into pans."

"Oh, goody."

The screen door slammed, and Penny turned to Marny, who was coming around the back of the car. "That takes care of them," she said, as she put her arm around Marny's waist. "It's hotter than the hammers for Labor Day, so let's go in and have some iced tea while we sample Minna's fresh-baked cookies."

"Mums," Parri said, unable to bear the new turn of events a moment longer, "Marny's a junior."

"She is? Good for her."

"She'll be sixteen this month," Parri went on, trying to convey a message as they went up the steps to the porch.

"Lucky girl." Penny swiped an arm over her brown hair, which was tied on top of her head with a shoestring she had filched from her husband, and said to Marny, "I wish I could be sixteen again. Parri, who will reach the ripe old age of seventeen next month, hasn't much longer to enjoy it. Minna," she called through a gaping window that opened into the kitchen, "the newest member of our family has come."

Parri knew that in a subtle way she was being admonished. "Sixteen, seventeen," her mother's cheery statement had implied, "there isn't much difference between them, so stop being stuffy. If Marny is only eleven months younger than you are, accept it and be gracious.

"There was a telephone call from your Aunt Tippy," Penny went on to Marny, flopping into a rattan chair with flowered cushions, and looking almost as young as the two who sat down across the porch from her. "They'll try to get back here to lunch, but if they shouldn't, you're to wait for them. Oh, thanks, Minna."

Glasses of iced tea were being passed through the window by a comfortably upholstered woman in a blue-and-white-striped dress. To Marny, who sprang up to take them, she looked a little like the matron at The Home, in a pleasant Swedish way.

"Minna," Penny said, "this is our newest niece. Marny, this is Minna Thompson, John's wife. Without these two, Round Tree Farm couldn't run.

"How do you do, Mrs. Thompson," Marny said politely, missing the withering look Parri directed at her back.

"Just call me Minna," the voice inside the window said, and out came a plate of cookies. "Tippy Two, she is gone to take a basket of refreshments to Petey and John. Do you want anything else, ya?"

"Another glass of tea for me," a voice said from inside, and Marny knew it belonged to her Uncle Josh. It had to be his, in this house. And when the man with the keen eyes and furrowed cheeks whom she remembered from last night came out to smile at her and give her shoulder a pat, she smiled unselfconsciously back at him.

She liked this family. She liked it, she thought, next to the Jordons, or perhaps equally with the Parrishes who were so rich that they had been harder to know. The Mac-Donalds were no doubt rich, also. Aunt Tippy had said they were, or would be if they would stop putting their money back into other theatrical enterprises. They worked hard, but so did Uncle David and Uncle Bobby, so she assumed that Aunt Carrol was the only really rich one.

She listened to the conversation flowing around her, watched Parri hop up to take a telephone call that turned out to be for her father; and when forty-five minutes had passed, asked anxiously, "Do you think Petey and Tippy Two are all right? Perhaps I should go and see about them."

"Oh, they're fine," Parri answered, before either parent could. "If they wander over to the pool, Joshu and a bunch of his friends are out there."

Marny was sure that this pool would be different from the wading pool in Atlanta. It would be as big as the one in the high school gymnasium, and Petey couldn't swim. Tippy Two could, a little, her mother had said, in a dog-paddling fashion that kept her afloat, so she was anxious. Even while everyone talked, she could hear boys' shouting voices in the distance, but not the shrill pipes she listened for. And when her Aunt Penny suggested, "Why don't you take Marny out and show her the pool, Parri?" she set her glass on the table and promptly stood up.

Parri was slower to follow. She knew the children were safe, wherever they were, and as they walked along a path through the trees that seemed interminable to Marny, she asked, "Would you like to take a swim?"

"I didn't bring my bathing suit," Marny said, thinking of her new pink and white lastex suit back at the motel. But Parri answered carelessly:

"Oh, we have plenty of suits in the dressing rooms. If you *really want to.* . . ."

"I don't." Marny didn't. She knew that Parri didn't either, and when she saw the pool with six shouting boys playing water polo in it, she understood why.

There was no sign of the children, but she could hear their reassuring voices coming from a vegetable garden behind a two-storied garage.

"This is it," Parri said, waving her hand to encompass three dressing-room doors, an open kitchen, and a screened dining area, all under one long roof. Then she wondered what they could do next. Tippy Two and Petey were safe, Marny could hear that as well as she could, and they had so little in common to talk about.

"Don't inquire into her past," was another thing her mother had cautioned that morning. "If Marny wants to tell you about it, she will." So here they were, with nothing to do.

"I hope Aunt Tippy will find a house for you all," she said, clutching at the only subject she could safely discuss, and starting back the way they had come.

"Oh, I do, too." Marny's eyes shone with anticipation, then she laughed. "You said 'you all' just the way we do down south!" she exclaimed. "I wouldn't want to be back there, but it sounded so natural to hear it. Southerners say 'you all' when they may mean just you. They have a lot of different expressions."

"I know." Parri decided that they might sit down under a tree for a time; so, stopping at a group of slatted wooden chairs around a table, she said, "Aunt Tippy called everyone 'sugar' last night. Up here we say 'honey' and down there you say 'sugar.'"

"Yes, we do." Marny picked up a leaf that had left its mother tree too early and floated down to land on the seat of a chair; and twirling its stem between her thumb and forefinger, she sat down and asked, "You don't think I talk funny, do you?"

"You drawl your words a little," Parri answered, and to her surprise she found herself adding, "It doesn't sound funny. It sounds sort of pretty."

"I hope I lose it," Marny said earnestly. "I don't want to be one bit different from the rest of you. I practiced all the way up here and I thought I had it licked. Last night," she confided, "I noticed that the aunt who wants me to call her Bitsy spoke with a slight British accent."

"That's because she lived in England during her childhood, with Uncle Peter's sister."

"Oh, yes, I know all about her," Marny supplied. "She's Aunt Jenifer, and I've seen pictures of her and her husband and her two children. It's wonderful," she said joyously, "to have so many ready-made uncles and aunts. Why, just think, Parri, they've been here waiting for me all my life, and I didn't know it. It would have helped a lot if I could have known it. But perhaps it's better this way," she said philosophically. "It would have made me too impatient for this time to come, and I'd have kept myself in a tizzy trying to picture what it would be like. This way, every day is an exciting surprise. Tell me," she asked, resting her sandals on the wooden rim of the chair seat and hugging her bare knees, "do you ever feel all fluttery inside? Just from pure happiness?"

"Why, sometimes I do," Parri answered, surprised. "When something's coming up that I'm awfully keen about."

"Oh, I mean all the time. I feel sort of like this leaf,"

Marny tried to explain, still twirling the fragile green stem. "It has always lived bunched in with a lot of other leaves, and I think it's a little dizzy from floating down here to me. That's the way I feel, dizzy and free." She stopped because Parri was regarding her strangely. Then she hunched her shoulders and laughed. "I'm not a nut," she said, "or if I am, I'm a happy nut. I think all these thoughts are bursting out of me because you're the youngest one I've had to talk to. The youngest one I've *ever* had to talk to—even though you're lots older than I am."

"I'm not so much older," Parri heard herself admit. "Just eleven months."

"You seem older. You drive a car, and you knew just how to come back at Lang last night when he was teasing me. I didn't." Marny carefully put the leaf in the pocket of her white shirt and said, "Yet, in some ways you seem younger."

"How?" Parri asked, discovering that she liked Marny far more than she had thought she could.

"Well, you're so carefree. I can't explain it very well but. . . ."

"Don't tell Davy that," Parri interrupted, grinning wryly. "He'd back you up a hundred per cent. He thinks I'm practically a moron. That is, he did until I agreed to stay home and run the house this winter. I'm learning to be more responsible, Marny, the way you've had to be. Perhaps, if you can learn to be as carefree as you think I am and I can learn to be as reliable as I know you are, we'll turn out to be a couple of perfect girls. There's one other thing you'll have to do, though. You'll have to smile more."

"I'll try," Marny promised, pressing the leaf flat in her

pocket. "I do when I'm with Aunt Tippy and Uncle Major because they make me feel so happy. It's almost unbearable to be so happy," she said with an ecstatic sigh, before she remembered to widen her mouth into a broad grin.

They sat talking companionably under the shading tree, and, contrary to her mother's warning, Parri learned a great deal about Marny's past. It came in bits and pieces, with Marny springing up now and then to look anxiously at a truck parked beside the vegetable garden, and with Parri scolding her about her overprotectiveness.

"Parrish and Jordon kids have all managed to grow up," she said the last time, when Marny was watching the truck bounce along a rutted road that would bring it into a grove of trees beyond the driveway. "Sit down and listen while I tell you about some friends of mine who are coming over to swim this afternoon. One of them is Alan Moseby. He's in college and is a very special friend."

"I know about him," Marny said; and having made certain that the children were all right, she dropped back into her chair. "Aunt Tippy told me. You call him Mose, and his father is an army officer, stationed at West Point. Mose works for Uncle Bobby at his automobile agency in the summer, pumping gas and helping in the repair shop. He wants to go into the diplomatic corps when he graduates.

"Good gracious, you do know a lot about us." Parri said. blinking. "What else do you know?"

"Not too much. I know that Davy is in love with Bitsy, but Bitsy may be in love with Keith Drayton who was Aunt Alcie's brother-in-law before she was killed in the automobile accident. He's older than Davy, and has a good job with a chemical firm. And since Davy and Bitsy are just the same age, everybody thinks. . . ." An automobile horn shattered the quiet. Marny knew the sound of that horn. It belonged to Old Betsy; and she cried, "They're back! Let's go see if they've found us a house. Come on!"

They began to run across the grass, and, without thinking, Parri reached out to clasp Marny's hand in hers, so that they ran as a team.

"Darn it, we didn't find a single thing I'd live in," Tippy was saying when they were all on the porch, with Minna's arm coming through the window frame to dispense iced tea. "Not so far, at least." Then she turned to Penny to ask, "When Daddy Jordon phoned you a little while ago, did he say why he wants us to stop by his house?"

"No." Penny shook her head. "He just said that he hoped you'd come there to lunch. And when I told him that I'm feeding you here—quickly, so you can be on your way again—he said to be sure and have you stop by before you go on looking. That's all he said."

"He might have heard about something new," Peter put in, taking his empty glass back to Minna for a refill. "The old boy always plays golf on a holiday, so if he gave that up to wait for us, we'd better drop by there as soon as we leave here. Minna," he stuck his head through the window to ask, "how is the iced tea holding out?"

There was chuckling inside the kitchen, then a frosty pitcher was handed to him. And while he made the rounds with it, Marny leaned over Tippy's chair to whisper, "Parri is sure that Tippy Two and Petey are all right, but I just saw the truck go by and I don't know where John is taking them."

"Just around the house to the side yard," Tippy said.

"Don't worry about them. I saw John trimming the grass around a tree and he has two bothersome helpers. And at any rate, here they come with Joshu."

"This is to be a picnic lunch, but I don't know where we're all going to sit," Penny said, coming from the kitchen with a platter of cold meats surrounded by deviled eggs. "It's a good thing that Josh had to take off for town. Susan, you and Bobby can squash in around our small table with Parri, Tippy, Peter, Marny and me, and the kids can take to the breakfast room."

Tippy Two and Petey were already on their way, tagging after Joshu. Marny, seeing Minna bringing out a plate of sandwich bread and a bowl of salad, sprang up to take them from her.

Everyone chattered during the hurried meal except Tippy. She sat in silence. "I didn't see one house that was right for us," she said, when Penny snapped her fingers under her nose and told her to come back and join the party. "One of them was nice, but it was too far away. They all were, for that matter. I might just as well live in Atlanta. Peter," she asked, "do you think we could fit into that boxy little place we saw near Mums' and Dad's?"

"No," he answered. "Not unless you want to buy a sofa-bed for the living room and open it up every night."

"I don't."

"Perhaps the ones we'll see this afternoon will turn out to be better," Susan comforted. "We still haven't looked at the one Carrol heard about or the one Bobby is saving until last. Is it any good, Bobby?" she looked across the crowded table to ask.

Bobby Parrish had been unusually quiet during lunch, and now he said mysteriously, "I like it, but it might not suit Tippy at all. It's near the rest of us and I think's it's a peach of a house, but it is rather old."

"Ugh. I don't want an old crumbly place without Peter there to mend things that break," Tippy said, and she dropped all consideration of that house without inquiring further about it.

7

Penny decided to join the expedition after Bobby had insisted that she would enjoy it. Petey and Tippy Two were resting with Minna on guard, so she drove the station wagon and took Marny and Parri with her.

When the two cars turned in at Gladstone, Marny was surprised to notice a second driveway branching off from the main one just inside the gates. She knew General Jordon lived on the Gladstone acres, but yesterday she had been so busy looking at the great mansion in the distance that she hadn't noticed a tall white-stuccoed house. This one is certainly big and old, she thought, looking up at a circular tower on one end of the house. It looks like one of those castles in a fairy tale.

Then the car stopped and she walked with the others along a flagstoned path that was bordered on one side by a rose garden, and up some steps to a stone terrace enclosed by a stone balustrade. There were open French doors beyond it, and General Jordon was standing at the top of the steps.

"Come in, come in," he said genially. "I assume you've had your lunch."

"Penny fed us, Dad," Peter said, watching his father give Tippy a hearty hug. "What did you want to see us about?"

"If you'll all come in and sit down, I'll tell you."

He led the way into an unusually large living room with white plastered walls, dark woodwork, and a beamed ceiling. Comfortable chairs were scattered about, some slipcovered in a bright flowered fabric to match a long sofa that faced a fireplace. A big Oriental rug with smaller ones around it covered most of the polished hardwood floor, and there were tables with lamps on them. It was a restful room, and Marny wondered how it would be to live in it, dreaming away the hours in one of the recessed window seats, cozy on a dark red pad, and looking out through a mullioned casement window at snow or rain or sunshine.

"Now, everybody sit down," General Jordan brought her back to the present by saying. "Bobby, you take this chair; Peter, you take the one opposite him; girls, you three can sit on the sofa. That puts us in a group, and somebody can pull up a chair for me."

Each sat where he or she had been told to sit because it was natural to obey General Jordan. Marny and Parri, without direction, went off to perch side by side in one of the window seats. Peter got up again to bring a chair from across the room, and General Jordon seated himself with his back to the empty fireplace and faced his audience.

"I know you're wondering why I asked you to come over here in the heat of the day," he said, when they were all in place. "I did it because I have a problem."

"What sort of problem, Dad?" Peter asked, knowing that his father's life was perfectly organized. Since his retirement, he had been made an executive in a textile firm. He had a housekeeper; his health was excellent; and there were no children about now to disrupt his peaceful routine. He had no problems, so far as Peter could see.

"Well, son . . ." the General had to clear his throat before he could continue, ". . . I want to take a trip. In fact, I have my tickets." He patted the breast pocket of a light summer jacket he wore, then remembered that the tickets were in a desk drawer in his New York office. "I have my complete itinerary for a trip around the world," he said.

"Gee, Dad, that's swell!" Peter exclaimed, while the others answered with surprised nods.

"It's partly business and partly pleasure," General Jordon explained. "My firm wants me to go to a number of countries as a good-will ambassador and stir up sales. I started once, as you well remember, Susan." He had to stop for several embarrassed hur-rumphs, and Susan filled the pause by saying:

"Yes, Daddy, I remember. You took me with you, and you got the Asian flu in Hong Kong and we had to come back. That was when Bobby showed up and I discovered I was in love with him."

"Ah, yes. Bobby was very helpful," the General said, appreciative of his son-in-law who had been trailing Susan halfway around the world. "I might have died if Bobby hadn't been there to put all three of us on a plane for home." His lips twitched in a smile as he looked at Bobby, who grinned back proudly, then winked at Susan.

"However," the General went on, "I'm making the trip alone, this time. I expect to be gone six months."

"*Six months?*" Susan echoed.

"Six months. Bitsy says she may join me later, but that remains to be seen. Ellin plans to take a well-earned holiday to visit her relatives." Such a fit of throat-clearing seized him that afterward he was obliged to say, "Excuse me. This leaves me with a vacant house on my hands. It seems a waste, doesn't it?"

"I don't think so, Dad." Peter felt Tippy's disturbed eyes on him, so he said, "If you're cooking this up just to give us a home for a few months, it won't work. I'll be away for a year, maybe two, and I want to get Tippy settled somewhere that's permanent before I leave."

"Now, wait just a minute." There was a general stirring of interest from everyone but Bobby Parrish. Bobby, relaxed in his chair, grinned his foxy grin and waited. "You haven't heard all of it," General Jordon said, "so don't jump to conclusions, son, until you do."

He was so interested in his subject now that he forgot to clear his throat. "As you know," he explained carefully, "when Susan was married I deeded a piece of ground to her to build a house on: two acres. It was part of the land I had bought from Carrol when I first came here. I had never used it for myself because I was too comfortable here, and since then Carrol has assured me that she hopes I will stay on in Gladstone Gates indefinitely. That leaves me with eight acres: two for you, Peter, and two each for Neal, Vance, and Bitsy. My suggestion to you is that you build a house on your property and that Tippy and the children move into this one while it's going up. How does that strike you?"

"It's wonderful of you, Daddy Jordon," Tippy said gratefully, for both herself and Peter, "but you see, we can't do it. We're army, and we don't know where we'll be stationed when Peter comes back from Vietnam. We'd be left with an empty house on our hands."

"I figured that you might rent it," Bobby said, crossing one long leg over the other and looking very comfortable in his chair. "That way, it would pay for itself and you'd always have a home when you want it."

"Bobby Parrish," Tippy cried, sitting straight up and glaring at him, "you knew about this when you were dragging us from house to house this morning! You knew Daddy Jordon was planning to suggest this, and this house is the one you called rather old."

"You're right," he returned complacently. "Dad told me about it the other day, and I wanted you to see for yourself that there aren't any places to rent before he sprang it on you."

"Well, of all the mean tricks. Susan," Tippy turned her head to ask, "did you know about it, too?"

"No." Susan shook her head and said, "Bobby can be awfully mum when he wants to be, but I do think it's a perfect solution."

"Would you want *renters* living next door to you?"

"Of course," Susan replied. "With children—so Ti Me will have someone to play with. It sounds marvelous to me."

"Peter? What do you think?" Tippy looked at Peter, who only shook his head before he clasped his hands between his knees and leaned forward to say earnestly to his father, "Dad, I think it's the grandest thing I've ever heard of anyone doing for his kids, but we can't accept it. We can't afford to build a house," he pointed out. "Not the kind that ought to go up around here. Not one like Bobby's. We've got enough for the down payment, sure, but mortgage money is high and my paycheck is small. We're grateful, Dad, but it's out of the question."

An explosion of arguments in favor of building the house broke out; and Marny, listening from the window seat, whispered to Parri beside her, "Do you understand what it's all about? Is Uncle Major being persuaded to build the house or is he still turning it down? You know the family better than I do, so what do you think?"

"I can't tell, yet," Parri whispered back. "We'll have to wait and see." Then she heard a car pull into the driveway behind her and twisted around to look through the window. "Uh-oh," she said. "Here come Aunt Carrol and Uncle David. I'll bet you a nickel now that you'll build a house. Aunt Carrol will take over the mortgage the way she did for Uncle Bobby, and before Aunt Tippy and Uncle Peter know what's happened to them, a crew of workmen will be putting in their foundation."

"Does that mean that we'll move in here for a while?"

"Yes, but listen. Something else is happening."

She and Marny sat quietly in their secluded nook, watching the room. Nobody was sitting now. At first they surrounded David and Carrol; then a group transferred itself to Bobby, who was saying, "Look, Tip, you don't have to hire an architect, so stop talking about that expense. I happen to know a guy who's a builder. He has a lot of good stock plans, and because he's a friend of mine he agreed, as a personal favor to me, to start work right away. In fact, he's sitting in his office now, waiting for us. And here's one more thing you might consider," he said, as she still stared at him in bewilderment. "Peter's quite apt to come back and be stationed at West Point. Dad told me that."

"Is *he* pulling strings *too?*" Tippy asked, unable to believe that her father would meddle in his son-in-law's military career.

"No, the Superintendent of the Academy mentioned it to him. Peter is a graduate and a darned good officer, and he's on the list to come back as an instructor. That's routine, Tip. You could live on the post in crowded majors' quarters," he pointed out, "or you could live right in your own house with Peter drawing commutation."

"Oh." Tippy left Bobby so suddenly that he wondered if she had heard a word he was saying.

She had, and she went dashing across the room to Marny. "Listen, sugar," she said, "we're going to build a house, and Uncle Major and I have an awful lot to do. We're going to live here for a few months," she remembered to add, as if Marny hadn't heard everything. "Right now, we have to rush down to the builder's office to go over plans. I'm sure Bobby will want to take us there, so find someone to drive you back to look after the kids. Stay at Penny's until we come to pick you up." And she went flying off again.

"It looks as if your future is nicely settled," Parri said, standing up, ready to leave. "If we're to get home by the time my gang shows up, we'd better snag a ride." And when Marny still stood looking at the scene before her: at her Uncle Major off in a corner with Bobby, making figures on the back of an envelope; at her Aunt Tippy hugging

General Jordon; at the others still talking in an excited huddle, she urged, "Come on."

"Oh, I'm coming." Marny gave an excited gasp, and said, "See? It's like I told you. If I had tried to imagine this kind of future when I didn't know I had any future to imagine, I never could have imagined anything like this."

8

"Hi, all, I'm sorry I'm late," Parri called to three friends who sat on the porch, waiting for her. "Marny, this is Barbie Andrews," she introduced them, "and this is Dick Wicks—but we always call him Dicky-Wicky because he's such a clown—and this is Mose. Marny is my cousin and she's come up to live with Aunt Tippy this winter and go to school here."

"Charmed, I'm sure," Dick Wicks said, springing forward to make such an elaborate bow that had not Mose jerked him back by the belt of his chinos, his head would have banged into Marny, who was still coming forward.

Marny smiled shyly at each one. Barbie was a pretty

blonde who seemed colorless beside Parri. Mose looked much as she had thought he might; not as tall as she had pictured him, or as good-looking, but he had nice dark hair and level gray eyes. Dicky-Wicky, snub-nosed, red-haired, suited his nickname.

"Are we going to swim or not?" he asked Parri. "We've been sitting here panting for over half an hour."

"Ten minutes," Mose corrected. "This is my afternoon off, so I'm in no hurry. Dick's job ended yesterday, so he hasn't a thing to do all the rest of the week."

Marny noticed that he said Dick instead of Dicky-Wicky. She supposed it was because they were both in college. Yet, when Barbie and Mose picked up their canvas bags that held their bathing suits, and Dicky-Wicky's swimming trunks fell out of a sloppily rolled towel, she watched him pounce on them and spank them, wondering if he was ever serious enough to make passing grades.

"I think I'd better go and see if Tippy Two and Petey are all right," she said, as the others started toward the door. And she had to ask Parri, "How do I get upstairs?"

"You won't need to go." Parri looked up from reading a scrawled note she had found on the table, and said, "Joshu has taken them to the Simpsons' to play with a bunch of little kids. Minna said they could go, so it's all right. They just live up the road from us."

What a carefree family, Marny thought, reluctantly following the others outside. She didn't know who the Simpsons were or where to find their house, or if her Aunt Tippy would want the children to go there. They had been lost from her watchful care all morning, and now they were lost again.

"Are you sure the children are all right?" she asked Parri,

when they reached a dressing room and Parri had taken a red two-piece suit from a hook and handed it to her.

"Of course they are," Parri answered positively. "Mrs. Simpson is always around."

"But Petey's so little," Marny murmured, never having seen the Jordon children with any little friends.

"Relax. We'll walk down there after our swim if you still feel worried." Parri left Marny alone in the dressing room and went back outside to an umbrella-covered table, to sit down across from Mose.

He wore his swimming trunks with a towel draped around his neck, and he looked over at her to ask, "How's the cousin business going?"

"Better than I thought it would," Parri admitted. "Marny's kind of sweet. How did you like her?"

"She's older than I expected her to be," Mose said. "From what you told me I thought she was a *little* kid."

"She'll be sixteen next week, and a junior." Parri sighed and said, "She worries so much about Tippy Two and Petey. My goodness, you'd think she's a nursemaid or a baby sitter or something. She's so *trustworthy*."

"And you aren't, is that it?"

He grinned at her while he waited for her answer. And kicking off her sandals and sliding down in her chair to rest her bare feet on the table, she said, "No, thank goodness. I do what I have to do but I don't go to extremes about it. I know the kids are all right, so why stew and fuss?"

"But Marny doesn't know it," Mose pointed out. "She's never heard of the Simpsons. This is all strange stuff to her."

"Oh, don't be so righteous," Parri pouted. "You're almost as bad as Davy. In fact, you're worse." Then she grinned and wrinkled up her nose at him. "I guess that's why I like you," she said. "Maybe we *should* take a run up to the Simpsons', and check. I suppose Aunt Tippy would want me to. Will you drive me in your car?"

"Come on."

They were gone when Marny came out of the dressing room. She had pulled the narrow top of the bathing suit up and the shorts down as far as each would go, but in spite of all she could do it was a scanty costume and she wished she had her own pink suit. And she also wished she could swim as well as Barbie, who was cutting through the water in the pool with a long overhand stroke that kept her beside Dicky-Wicky. There was no sign of Parri and Mose, so she sat down in the chair Parri had vacated to wait for them.

It seemed to her that she had sat there for an uncomfortably long time before she saw them coming toward her through the trees, with Tippy Two and Petey walking silently between them.

"We brought them home," Parri called. "All the little Simpsons had gone to the supermarket with their mother, and these two had said they didn't have permission to go. We found them sitting forlornly on the steps. Can they swim?" she asked, as the children fled around the end of the pool to Marny as to a haven.

"Tippy Two can," Marny said, taking Petey on her lap and wiping away muddy tear streaks, "but they haven't their bathing suits."

"We thought we were lost," Petey whispered, learning back against her and covering up most of her bare midriff while Tippy Two added with the wisdom of eight:

"I kept telling him that somebody would come and get us, but he wouldn't listen. He was a great big baby. He cried."

"I did not!" Petey lifted his head to shout. "I just wanted to come home."

"Well you're here now, so everything is all right," Marny told him, hugging him closer. And she looked up to say, "Thanks, Parri, for bringing them back."

"Thank Mose," Parri said airily. "He's the one who took me."

"Thank you, Mose." Marny sent Mose a glad, relieved smile that quirked up the corners of her mouth and gave her solemn little face an impish look.

Why, she's pretty, he thought, dropping into a chair beside her. She could provide the local gals with some competition if she wanted to. Maybe it's a lucky thing that she's younger than they are. And he asked her, "How do you like it here, Marny?"

"Oh, I love it," Marny answered around Petey's head, as she had grown accustomed to doing ever since they had started north, either around his or Tippy Two's, or both. "Every day is nicer than the one before it."

She was content, now that she had half of the family with her, and she became brave enough to put on the swimming cap Parri gave her and to make a passable dive into the pool. It was five o'clock when Mose took Barbie and Dicky-Wicky off in a car that Parri said had been his birthday gift last year and she heard the welcome sound of the horn she knew so well. She had enjoyed the afternoon. It was another first to put in the memory book of her mind, but she was eager now to go back to the motel and hear more about the new house they were to build.

"We brought three plans home with us," Tippy said, when, barefooted, they were all sitting on one of the twin beds in the motel room, with Switzy enjoying his bowl of supper on a newspaper. "None of them suits us exactly because I want a *wide* living room instead of a long narrow one, and we need a family room, or a library or something, where we can really live. I got awfully tired of trying to pick up the clutter in Georgia and keeping the one living room neat."

"But we don't want it down in the basement where this house has it," Peter said, unfolding an architect's blueprint of the house they liked best. "We'd never go down there."

He and Tippy bent over the plan together, and Marny, from the foot of the bed, had only an upside-down view of a stiff sheet of blue paper that had meaningless white lines crisscrossing each other.

"I want to go to Grandma and Grandpa's now," Tippy Two said, when both parents were running their fingers along the lines. "I'm hungry."

"Oh, good gracious!" her mother cried, scrambling off the bed and stumbling over Switzy's bowl, which was fortunately empty. "We're supposed to be there at six o'clock for dinner! Hurry, everybody!"

They were only fifteen minutes late when they pulled in at the Parrish driveway, and Marny had an unobstructed view of the white house with bay windows. Colonel and Mrs. Parrish were waiting for them on a small centered portico, and Trudy, the thin dearly loved Negro woman who had been with them for over forty years, came hobbling out.

"Oh, Trudy, darling," Tippy cried, hugging her, "I didn't get a chance to come over and see you today, but Mums says your arthritis is better. Is it?" she asked anxiously.

"It is, child, it is," Trudy answered, holding on to both her and Peter for safety when the exuberant Tippy Two and Petey hurled themselves at her. "It seems mighty good to have my little family back again. Is this our Marny?" she asked, freeing one hand so she could draw Marny closer. "Why, she looks like our Miss Alcie," she said in surprise, turning back to Tippy. "No wonder you took to her so fast. You always loved our little Alcie so much."

"Why, I hadn't thought of that!" Tippy exclaimed. "Marny *does* look a lot like Alcie. She has the same big gray eyes, and the brown bang. . . . She *does* look like Alcie, doesn't she, Peter?"

"Yes, I've noticed it," Peter agreed soberly, "but I didn't mention it. She's a lot like Alcie in her ways, too. You see," he explained to Marny, "Alcie was my sister whom we all loved so much. She was your Aunt Tippy's dearest friend, too, and she was killed last year in an accident."

"I know about her," Marny said softly, "and I'm awfully proud that I remind you of her."

"You do," Colonel and Mrs. Parrish said together; and Mrs. Parrish added, "Come inside, dears. Trudy and I have been preparing for this all afternoon. We're having fried chicken and the very special fruit salad Peter likes, and chocolate ice cream for Tippy Two and Petey."

"Wow!" Petey shouted, and was first through the door.

Marny loved the house. It was so cool and friendly. There was a small foyer with a stairway going up from it. It had a dining room on one side, and a living room on the other, as large and wide as her Aunt Tippy wanted hers to be, with a screened porch beyond it.

"Let's go out on the porch," she heard Colonel Parrish

suggest; and as she pushed Petey before her, she watched Tippy Parrish Jordon look about her like a daughter who had come home.

Tippy helped Trudy through the dining room to the kitchen, and when her mother would have followed, she stopped to call back, "Now, you stay and listen to Peter tell about the big day we've had. Trudy and I know what we're doing, and we don't want anyone messing in. That includes you, Miss Tippy Two. You and Petey can go down by the brook, but don't fall in. I didn't bring a change of clothes. Marny," she remembered to add, "if grown-up talk bores you, you can go along and investigate with them. We'll call you when we're ready."

There was little to do in the modern, well-organized kitchen. Tippy, taking platters and vegetable dishes from their places in the well-remembered cabinets, said, "Trudy, I know the telephone has been buzzing all afternoon, so do you think we're doing the right thing in letting the family stake us to a house?"

"Yes, child, I do," Trudy answered, bending over the oven as Tippy had seen her do through all her life. "You've got to remember that the Parrishes are different from a lot of folks, and the Jordons are, too. Bobby, our harum-scarum one, would never have gotten a start and found himself without them. We're a family, Tippy, child, and this is our God-given opportunity to bring you back into it. We don't have the money Miss Carrol has, or even Penny, but all of us are wanting to help, so just appreciate and accept. That's all you have to do."

"I see that," Tippy said, going over to take the pan of fried chicken from the warming oven before Trudy could lift it. "I realized it today. Peter and I are so used to living far away from you all and being independent that we didn't want to be—I used your word when I told Peter how I felt —we didn't want to be 'beholden.' ''

"Everybody is beholden," Trudy said. "That little Marny you took is beholden to you, and she's happy about it. She plans to pay her way by giving you happiness. You're giving us happiness. Isn't that enough for you?"

"It should be." Tippy took the salad from the refrigerator, then said, sniffing it, "This smells delicious. To give and to share. That's happiness, Trudy."

"Yes'm." Trudy held out the electric beater and pointed to a pan of boiled potatoes on the stove, saying, "Now, you just mash those like you'd mash your worries into a mound of pleasure, and you'll make yourself a meal that'll last you a lifetime. We're about ready to call the folks to the table, child."

It was a happy family gathering. Marny felt it more keenly than she had the night before when there had been so many people around such a sumptuous banquet table. Petey waved a drumstick, and when it flew out of his hand to land on the floor, he crawled under the table to find it without anyone laughing or commenting on it.

Everybody hopped up and down to change the empty plates; Switzy was fed choice bits; and after the dishes were done and Trudy had been helped up the stairway to her room, Marny stopped Tippy in the foyer to say, "Aunt Tippy, I love this house. Of course, I love the people in it, and the house seems to suit them. Aunt Carrol's is so grand, and of course I didn't see much of Parri's, just the kitchen and porch, and I haven't been in Aunt Susan's, yet. General Jordon's was big and different, but this one is the nicest house I've ever been in. It looks like you, Aunt Tippy."

Tippy stared at her for several seconds before she cried, "You angel!" Then she went dashing through the living room to the porch. "This is going to be our house," she announced.

"I hope you're not planning to take it away from us," her father returned with pretended alarm. "We're quite attached to it."

"Oh, not this one," Tippy told him scathingly. "We're going to build one exactly like it. Peter," she asked, sitting down on the arm of his chair, "couldn't we duplicate this house?"

"Why, sure, if you want to," he said. "If we had the plans, that is." And he asked Colonel Parrish, "Do you have them, Dad?"

"We may. As you both know, David and Carrol and Penny and Josh gave us this house. They bought it for us while I was wounded and in the hospital, and they had all our furniture moved in by the time I came out. They added the garage and Trudy's room and bath above it. And later, when we put on the porch, I remember David saying that he had kept the builder's original plans, in case we should ever need new heat or new wiring. But wouldn't this house be too small for you?" he asked.

"It would be exactly right," Tippy said eagerly. "You have four bedrooms, and that's what we need; and instead of having this porch, we could make a second living room of it, and we could always build above it if we ever need to enlarge. Let's call David. Let's call the builder, let's call everybody right away! Oh, Marny, thank heaven for you!"

She was to say that many times during the two weeks before Peter had to leave.

General Jordon, looking happy and pleased, left on Wednesday for his round-the-world tour. Ellin, looking as if she were being sent off to prison, went to visit the relatives whom she hadn't seen in years. Peter and Susan drove them to the airport in her new car, one to take a plane for London, the other for Jacksonville, Florida.

"Dad strode aboard in a true military manner," Peter reported when he came back to find his family already moved in, with Tippy sitting on the high terrace as if she had always lived there, "but I almost had to push the old girl on her plane. She's afraid we'll neglect Cassius and Plush."

"Oh, she couldn't be." Tippy looked down at the brown frowsy dog that was lying at her feet, contentedly wagging a plumy tail that never seemed to stop wagging except when he slept, then at the black-and-white cat that had already leaped from the rail to settle on Peter's lap. "I promised Ellin that we'd take good care of them," she said, reaching down to pet Cassius, so making his tail thump even faster. "Switzy thinks Cas is another Rollo, and he lets Plush eat out of his bowl. She wasn't serious, was she?"

"Oh, not about the pets. They were just an excuse, but don't be surprised if she's back before Dad is. We've been her family for so long that relatives don't mean much to her. You see, Tip," he said, stroking Plush's shiny black fur that had given him his name, "Vance means more to her than any nephew she's going to meet, even though he is a first classman and doesn't bother to come home very often now. Tell me," he asked, "did you get moved in all right without me?"

"We most certainly did," Tippy answered proudly. Then, deciding that Cassius had had enough family love, she leaned back comfortably to say, "You had put all the suitcases upstairs for us, and I gave Marny Susan's old room —the tower room, you know—and Tippy Two has Bitsy's room because Bitsy said she'd rather have Ellin's room downstairs when she comes out on weekends. Petey has the one across the hall that used to be Neal's, next to Vance's cubbyhole that he likes, and I took your father's big room and bath for us. A very agreeable expressman brought in the trunks and boxes, and I left those in the upstairs hall until we need them. Then we had lunch. A very fine lunch, I must add," she said. "Ellin had left us, as Bitsy would say, 'with a well-stocked larder.' When we finished and the kids were just too excited to rest, Marny, bless her heart, walked them over to Gladstone."

The days went on. An excavating firm trucked in its bull-dozers to dig a great hole in the center of the land that General Jordon had deeded to them. "Don't injure the roots on that tree," Tippy or Peter would shout, climbing over mounds of earth to fling protective arms around a par-ticularly fine oak they wanted to save. "Move farther to the left and take those saplings if you have to." They were afraid to leave their site for fear a careless operator might ignore his pegged boundary and crash into one of their precious trees. And when, tired and mosquito-bitten, they drove home, Marny always had cool drinks and dinner ready for them.

"Thank heaven for you," Tippy said on Sunday evening, when the excavation was finished and the bulldozers had departed to tear up someone else's land. "Do you know that you start school tomorrow? Sylvester will drive Tippy Two to Briarcliff with Carli, and the kindergarten bus will pick up Petey. Is Parri coming for you?"

"She said she would," Marny answered. "If her mother needs the station wagon, she said John would take us, then come back for us. Aunt Tippy," Marny said, frowning, "I don't want Parri to feel that she has to drag me everywhere with her. I can ride with Tippy Two and Carli to the cross-roads, and then catch the school bus."

"We'll work it out." Tippy nodded understandingly. She knew that Marny wasn't the "beholden" type any more than she was. And she said, "If Old Betsy weren't so decrepit I'd see that you have driving lessons right after your birthday. I could use Daddy Jordan's car except on weekends when Bitsy may want it."

Marny secretly dreaded the first day of school, but she didn't say so. She looked like other girls now, but, feeling that she had so little to offer, she was timid about meeting them. The boys? She gave no thought to the boys. She had never known any boys, so they had no place in her life. It was the girls she worried about. Girls, who with happy lives and friends of their own, like Parri, might not notice a new student in their midst. She made no mention of her fear, however, but only dressed on Monday morning, and went downstairs as usual.

"Hi, Parri, I'm ready," she called, running down the side steps when Parri pulled up in the foreign car she had driven to the motel that first morning.

She wore her candy-striped dress that was her favorite; and as she got in and closed the door, she said, "It's awfully nice of you to come all the way over here to take me to-day."

"Oh, it wasn't much out of my way, "Parri replied, shifting gears. "I'll turn you over to Karen. She's the girl you met at my house the other day, and she'll introduce you around. I meant to invite some other girls out," she explained apologetically, "but I didn't know any other juniors you'd like."

"Oh, that's all right." Marny settled her purse on her lap. It held the money to buy her schoolbooks, and a little notebook in which she carefully entered every cent that her Aunt Tippy and Uncle Major paid out for her. When one of the two states responsible for her sent them a check, she would repay them.

"That's the high school," Parri said, when they reached town and were passing a long two-storied building that took up two square blocks. "I'll drive around to the students' parking lot and we'll go in a back door; then I'll find Karen for you."

The tight lump of nervousness in Marny's chest grew into a hard round ball, but she meekly followed Parri through corridors where Parri greeted students with a passing "Hi," and hurried on.

They couldn't find Karen, even though Parri looked in the home rooms where juniors should be, and when it was almost time for school to begin, she said, "I'd better take you to the principal's office. You'll have to go there anyway to register. Did Aunt Tippy tell him you're coming?"

"Yes, she did," Marny managed to answer. "She telephoned that my transcript would be sent to him, but I don't know if it has been."

"Well, there's the door to his office, right along this hall where you see a lot of kids going in and out," Parri said, relieved to be turning over her responsibility to someone in authority. "We'll be out of here by noon today, so come to the car when you're ready."

"Thanks a lot, Parri," Marny said gratefully. And, squaring her shoulders, she took her place in a long waiting line.

9

"Aunt Tippy, Aunt Tippy," Marny called, leaping up the steps to the terrace where Tippy was lying on the glider, drinking a Coke. "It went just fine!"

"I'm so glad." Tippy sat up and put her glass on a small table before her. "Tell me about it."

"Well," Marny said, laying a stack of schoolbooks on a table and dropping into a chair, "I was scared green at first."

"Oh, sugar, I didn't know you were," Tippy interrupted the recounting to say.

Marny grinned and said, "I didn't want to admit it to myself, but I was. And then everyone was so *helpful* to me. A teacher took me to a room that she said was to be my home room, and since all the other students were sitting at desks by then, she introduced me to them by saying, 'This is Marian Alexander, a new girl. I hope you'll make her feel welcome.' And they *did*, Aunt Tippy, they did! One girl, whose name is Lou Anne Willis, patted an empty desk across the aisle from her and said, 'Sit here by me, Marian, until we're assigned our regular seats.' So I did. Different ones took me to the classrooms where I was supposed to go and to a room where they were selling secondhand books. I bought what I needed there because I don't see any reason to spend good money for new books. And then, since the junior class finished before the senior class did, Lou Anne took me to a little shop down the street where I bought fillers for the notebook covers I have left over from last year, and a ballpoint pen, and a couple of pencils. Then I went back to the car and waited for Parri.

"Lou Anne is an awfully cute girl," she said, her eyes shining with the happiness of having found friends. "Her brother graduated last year and knows Parri. I never did see Karen," she said without rancor, "but it didn't matter. I got along just fine."

"And you liked it."

"Oh, I loved it," Marny said. "All the kids were calling me Marny by the time I left and it was the happiest school day I've ever had." Then she asked, "Where are Tippy Two and Petey?"

"At Carrol's. They came home almost as full of enthusiasm as you are, and Petey was blowing a whistle that some child had given him. Tippy Two had books—new ones, because she wasn't as frugal as you were—and Petey brought home a red cat he had colored. They've gone off to play school with Carli. Have you had your lunch?" she asked.

"No, but I'm not hungry. I invited Parri to come in and have lunch with me, but she said she had to go home because her mother and father are leaving tomorrow."

"Oh, so they are. I'll drive over there if Uncle Major ever gets back. He went off to meet Bobby and see about a change I want made in the kitchen cabinets, and that's the last I've seen of him all morning. I hope Old Betsy didn't get cantankerous and balk somewhere."

They both laughed because Old Betsy was given to fits of uncontrollable depression. Then Tippy saw a car turn in between the gateposts, and sat up. "Now, who could that be?" she said wonderingly.

It was a shiny new car, long and green, and when it branched off into their driveway, they could see Peter's face behind a closed window. "For heaven's sake, where did he get *that*?" Tippy cried, as Marny turned to look with her. Then she flew down the steps. "Peter Jordon," she called as she ran, "you haven't gone and done it, have you?"

"It's my parting gift to myself," he answered, getting out of the car to hug her. "I bought it so I won't have to sit in some rice paddy worrying about Old Betsy falling apart with you on a back road."

"You know we can't afford it," she scolded, looking at him instead of at the car that shone enticingly at her. "You had to move us up here where you knew I wanted to be so you wouldn't worry. You had to build us a new house so you wouldn't worry. Now you buy me a new car so I can ride elegantly around and you won't have to worry. You do everything for me and put it on the basis of pleasing yourself. You can take this right back," she cried, before he could speak. "It's just like Bobby to talk you into something like this!"

"He didn't talk me into it, Tip," Peter said, lightly kissing the dimple that looked as if it might never smooth out again. "He felt that everybody in the family is doing more for us than he and Susan can afford to do, so he sold me the car at cost, and gave me a whale of a turn-in on Old Betsy. He also arranged for a nominal, low-cost financing loan at his bank."

"*He did?*" Tippy let herself look at the car now. She inspected it from its heavy front bumper to its fancy rear lights, then left him to walk around it. "It has beautiful upholstery," she said, coming back to him, "and I suppose it has a motor under its hood, since you got here in it."

"A good one. This isn't Bobby's most expensive model," he told her, opening the driver's door, "but it has all the trimmings. If you'll seat yourself inside, Mrs. Jordon, I'll show you."

Tippy slid gingerly behind the wheel; and when Peter leaned in to start the motor, a blast of cold air hit her. "You nut," she shrieked, "you've bought *air conditioning!* We won't need it in winter."

"But we do right now and we will again next summer. When *I* come home from Vietnam," he said with teasing emphasis, "I don't plan to ride along fighting flies and mosquitoes."

"Oh, when you come home from Vietnam," Tippy scoffed, leaning out to put her arms around his neck. "You precious liar, you know you did it for us. It will be fall again by the time you get home. Oh, Peter, it's no wonder I love you." And after she had given him a tender kiss, she touched her lips to his forehead, his chin, and to each cheek before she straightened up to call, "Marny, come look at the new car Uncle Major has bought us."

Marny took the steps in two leaps, and the three stood gazing rapturously at their beautiful dream on wheels. "Want to try it out?" Peter asked; but Marny answered quickly:

"You go with him, Aunt Tippy. I'll make myself a sandwich, then walk over to Gladstone for Tippy Two and Petey. I'm so excited today that I won't know if I'm moving along on my own two feet or skimming over the ground in a helicopter."

The next three days were filled with happiness. Marny and the two little Jordons went off to school: Petey in his kindergarten bus, and Marny driven by Sylvester to the crossroads. Tippy met her there every afternoon, saying each time, "After we move, sugar, you'll only have to walk up the lane." Then, on Friday, Peter had to leave.

"You be good kids and help your mother and Marny," he said, standing on the terrace, after an early breakfast around the kitchen table where Jordons had always liked to have it. Then he stooped down and took both children in his arms. "I love you," he said tenderly, looking at each one." You're very dear to me." And in a lighter tone, he added, "I've got your pictures in my wallet, and I'm going to show them to every guy I meet." He kissed them and managed to stand up with them clinging to him when he put an arm around Marny. "We're grateful for you, honey," he said huskily. "Don't ever forget that. You're the one who can keep your Aunt Tippy happy."

"I will," Marny promised, trying not to cry. "Uncle Major . . ." her voice broke and she had to catch a deep breath before she could finish ". . . thank you for all you've done for me."

Tippy drove him to the airport in the new car. Marny

saw the children off to their separate schools, then waited for Parri, who had offered to drive her today. For the first time since school had started the hours dragged. Was Aunt Tippy home alone, crying? she worried. And when her school bus stopped at the crossroads, she was the first one off and ready to run the half-mile that would take her home. But Tippy was waiting there in the new car, as usual.

She had Tippy Two and Petey in the back seat, and, sounding just as she always had, she said, "Hop in. Uncle Major got off all right. He's going to telephone us from San Francisco this evening and every evening until he leaves for Saigon, so I think we should drive by the new house and see what progress they've made today. We just might have good news to report."

Marny searched her Aunt Tippy's face for traces of tears, but could find none. Parrish women had told their husbands good-by in five major wars, and both Parrish and Jordon men were accustomed to going off to fight for their country's ideals.

The house went up. It became a shell with gaping holes where windows would eventually be. September slipped into October; leaves, flushed red from frosty nights and tired from waving through the hot summer months, fluttered down to the ground to rest.

"Here's news about me, I think," Marny cried, one Saturday morning, when she had raced back from the post-box at the gate to find Tippy mending Petey's new jacket before a wood-burning fire in the living room. "The letter is addressed to you, and it's from the Welfare Board, not Miss Wilcox. Oh, Aunt Tippy, read it quickly."

Tippy tore open the envelope and a check dropped into her lap. "Good gracious, you're still Georgia's ward," she said, glancing at the check before she unfolded an enclosed note that was signed by Doris Wilcox. "What a tempest in a teapot. All we have to do," she said, scanning the lines, "is to give her a monthly report on your welfare, which we've been doing. I've already written her a long, long letter."

"And I've written her three," Marny said eagerly, "telling her how happy I am, and I wrote one to Mrs. Bullock."

"Then that takes care of that for the time being," Tippy said, thoughtfully rubbing her cheek, "but I don't think you're going to save much out of this month's check. You have to have a new winter coat. It's getting too cold for your yellow one, and you need skirts and sweaters, and boots, and—oh, gosh, Marny," she said, laughing, "you are now almost broke."

"That's all right by me." Marny sat down on the sofa, and with her feet tucked under her, she said, "Maybe we can squeeze out enough for Petey and Tippy Two's snow-suits, too."

"We can try." Tippy appreciated Marny's generous gesture, and she waved the check, saying, "Your needs are all taken care of, sugar, but this good fortune makes me realize that we haven't done much about Senator Robinson's son."

"We've sent lots of boodle up to him and Davy," Marny reminded, having learned that boodle to a West Pointer means cakes and cookies and homemade candy, and hoping that the Senator would consider that enough.

"But we haven't invited him here or even gone up to see him."

"I went." Marny hopped up to put another log on the fire before she said, "Parri drove me up to show me West Point, but we couldn't find either John or Davy. Davy was practicing with the football squad, and John was in a meeting somewhere. The third roommate—I mean the third wife—told the desk sergeant where they were. I saw a lot of West Point, but I didn't see John or Davy."

"Well, it doesn't matter. Carrol says he'll be home this Sunday, and I'll ask him to bring John with him and come over here." Tippy put the check back into its envelope, sure that the two busy cadets would have something more interesting to do than to spend a few dull hours with a "war widow" and her young family, and that if they came, it would be a very short and dutiful call.

Marny dreaded it. Not meeting John—he was only a name to her—but meeting Davy. Davy, from all she had heard from Parri, was an uncompromisingly virtuous young man. "Davy disapproves," "Davy thinks," "Davy would never do. . . ." To Marny, Davy Parrish was equipped with a bright shining halo that he never took off. He was the Untouchable.

So, when, on Sunday afternoon, she heard a rumble of male voices in the living room, she almost crept down the stairway at her Aunt Tippy's call. She had put on her new red knitted dress, not to impress Davy, just to give herself confidence.

Two cadets in gray uniforms were standing side by side with their backs to a glowing fire, and she knew instantly which one was Davy Parrish. He was the tall blue-eyed blond one who looked like his father. The other one, shorter, dark, with heavy eyebrows that almost met above his nose in a perpetual frown, would be John. He was scowling at her as she came along the room; then he jerked on a smile that made him look less ferocious.

"This is our Marny," Tippy said proudly from the sofa, and they both stepped forward.

"Hi, Marny," Davy said, taking her hand and even adding a cousinly pat on the back, while John offered a stiff, "How do you do?"

"Hello. I do just fine," Marny answered seriously, "thanks to your father." And she managed a timid, "Hello, Davy."

She knew they were waiting for her to sit down somewhere; and in her hurry to do it, she folded up on the sofa and almost sat on Tippy. "Oh, mercy, excuse me," she said, sliding over a few inches and wrinkling up the short skirt of her red dress in the process. These guests weren't boys; they were men, she saw. And one of them was the great Davy. "It was nice of you to come over," she heard herself murmur; and to her relief they settled their stiff gray frames in two armchairs.

"Mom and Dad have told me a lot about you," Davy said easily, crossing one leg over the other in exactly the way his father and his Uncle Bobby did, and leaning back so that the front of his tight blouse bunched up a little.

My goodness, he shouldn't wrinkle, was all she could think of. Davy should never have a wrinkle in him. They were talking around her now, after having respectfully greeted her, and they didn't stay long. For that, she was grateful. Davy, when he was telling her good-by, said lightly, "I'll be seeing you now and then, Marny." And she tried to look at him as she answered untruthfully, "I hope so."

She didn't hope so at all. She hoped he would stay hidden in his gray stone fortress above the Hudson River. Davy scared her. She was sure he disapproved of her, as he disapproved of Parri, and would find some flaw in her character to pounce on. John didn't matter. She knew he had endured the brief call just as she had, and would be in no hurry to repeat it. It was that Davy.

She waited where she was while Tippy walked to the seldom-used front door with them, so didn't hear Davy say, "She's a nice kid, Aunt Tip, but gosh, she's a solemn little thing. Why don't you ask Parri to loosen her up?"

"Oh, Marny isn't solemn," Tippy denied, smiling. "She's serious, yes, too serious, I sometimes think, but she can be as animated as Parri, and over very small bits of happiness."

"Well, you know her better than I do," Davy said, bending to kiss her cheek before putting on his stiff gray cap. "Come on, John. We've paid a Sunday call and out we go into the last of the sunshine." He was standing on the steps when he remembered to say, "Bitsy won't be coming out to stay for a while, and with the football season under way, I won't be seeing you. Any boodle you care to send us will be appreciated."

"I'll remember. Good-by, boys, and thanks for coming over."

She watched them go along the curved walk to the driveway where Davy's car was parked, then closed the door and stood leaning against it. Was she making Marny too serious? she wondered, disturbed by Davy's remark. Was she neglecting Marny's social life with girls and boys her age? Had she kept her at home too much because she enjoyed being with her? Her conscience told her she had. So she went back into the living room, asking, "How did you like Davy and John?"

"They're all right," Marny answered, from her place on

the sofa. "Davy's about the way I thought he would be, and I decided that John isn't as cross as he looks."

"Well, they're too old for you." Tippy dismissed their recent guests, and sat down in the chair where Davy had sat to say brightly, "I think we should give a little party for you. We can invite some of your high school friends to a cookout before the weather gets too cold."

"Give a party?" Marny repeated, aghast. "Oh, Aunt Tippy, I don't want a party! I like things just the way they are."

"But, sugar, you need young friends. We live 'way out here in the country," Tippy tried to explain, "so all you do is go to school on the bus and come home again."

"That's what I want to do." Marny forgot her new red dress as she slid around on the sofa and leaned over its arm to say, "I'm so happy, Aunt Tippy. I guess you don't understand that there's nothing quite so wonderful to me as coming home. I go to school every day; I see kids I like and who like me, and then I come home. I'm making up all the years when I didn't have a home to come to. Why, every afternoon I can hardly wait for the bus to get here."

Her face was so alive now, so bright and happy, that Tippy wished Davy could see it. She even sprawled over the sofa arm as she flung out her hands to repeat, "I'm happy. I'm never lonesome or bored. I'm just happy."

"I'm glad of that." Tippy's conscience, like a courtroom lawyer, tried to say, "The defense rests," but she found herself still asking, "Wouldn't you like to have Lou Anne come out to spend the night sometime?"

"Goodness, no, I wouldn't know what to do with her. Oh, dear, I'm wrinkling my dress."

Marny bounced up to smooth out creases that might

have been there but weren't; and retying a belt that didn't need retying, she said, "You're sweet to suggest it, Aunt Tippy, but let's just go on the way we are. I love it this way." And she asked, "Is it time to go to Aunt Susan's and pick up Tippy Two and Petey now?"

"Almost. Come on, a walk along the footpath through the woods will do us both good."

The days went on, with Marny hopping off the school bus and running up the lane to the new house where she knew Tippy and the children would be, and with Tippy searching like a detective for any signs of boredom. "Darn you, Davy," she muttered now and then, when she watched Marny walk surefootedly along planks laid across the up-stairs joists where floors would soon be, guiding Petey before her while she led Tippy Two. "She is happy. I know it doesn't seem possible, but she is."

Often, when she had an errand in town, Tippy would leave the children at Susan's and pick up Marny after school. Because Marny was always told in advance, she would come running out to the curb where Tippy had parked. But one day in late October, arriving early, Tippy watched the town students pour out and saw Marny standing on the broad front steps, talking with a boy. Marny didn't look quite like Marny. She wore her new camel's-hair coat, but she was transferring her books from her arms to the boy's, and was looking up at him and laughing. Then they came down the steps together, and she suddenly stopped to scan the line of waiting cars as if a lasso had jerked her back.

Tippy forced herself not to call out. She only leaned over to run down the window, and waited. He was a nice-looking boy, she thought, studying him as they came toward her:

tall and skinny, as Peter had been at that age, but he had dark brown hair and bright brown eyes. Well, what do you know? she thought inadequately. Marny with a boy.

"Aunt Tippy," Marny said, when they reached the car, "this is Ron Carter. He's in my class at school."

"I'm sure glad to know you, Mrs. Jordon," Ron said quickly, leaning in the window and knocking a lock of hair over his forehead. "All Marny does is talk about her Aunt Tippy." And before Tippy could so much as get out "I'm glad to know you, too, Ron," he hurried on, "I've been trying to coax Marny to go to a home football game with me on Saturday. A bunch of us can pick her up, and afterward, we're going to eat at a pizza place we like. She says she won't go."

"Why not, sugar?" Tippy asked, thinking that here fell manna from heaven.

"I don't want to," Marny said, glaring, as nearly as Marny could glare, at Ron. "I've other things to do on Saturday."

"Now, what things?" Tippy questioned. "You're free as a bird on Saturday."

"No, I'm not. You forgot that you and Aunt Susan are going in to New York to look at wallpaper," Marny replied, prepared.

"Oh, pooh." Tippy poked her head through the window and risked colliding with Ron's as she said, "I can go any other day just as well. And if I do go then, we have a whole family of willing baby sitters. I think you should go to the game. Don't you, Ron?"

"You bet I do," Ron answered, grateful for her aid that, as in a Western, had arrived in the nick of time to save the fort. "I told Marny about the gang that will pick her up. Bev

Whitlock is going to take us—he's a senior and drives a car. He lives on the post at West Point and is bringing a girl from there, Allison Clark. I live out near you, too."

"You do? Then hop in and we'll drive you home." Tippy was not about to lose him. Not yet.

She watched him fling open the back door; and when Marny would have slid in beside her in front, she stretched across the seat to lay her hand protectively over the door handle. "Get in back with Ron," she prompted, to show Marny that that was the correct thing to do. "I'll be the chauffeur."

They rode through town, followed a highway for a mile or so, then turned off onto a curving country road; and when the silence behind her became so loud that it filled the car, she said, "You'll have to tell me where to take you, Ron."

"Oh, sure." He leaned over the front seat as if thankful to hear a spoken word, and said, "You go along just as if you're going to your house, but don't turn off at your road. Go on to the next one. I live in the first house this side of Parri's."

Carter? Carter? Tippy repeated mentally. And in surprised recognition of the name, she risked turning her head to say, "Why, I know who you are now. You're one of the Carter twins, aren't you? Your mother is a friend of Penny's."

"Um-hum. Hal and I used to play with Parri when we were little, but we're a year younger than she is, so she outgrew us."

"Now, isn't that amazing," Tippy said to Marny, as Ron sat back again. "We have a boy who is just your age living near us and we didn't know it."

146

"I knew it," Marny said flatly. "We take the same school bus."

"Sometimes she'll get on the bus and sit down beside me," Ron put in. "Not always, just sometimes. She likes to sit with a kooky little freshman."

"I help her with her math," Marny said defensively. "The poor kid doesn't understand it." And to Tippy's great relief, they began talking to each other.

"Well, here we are," she had to say too soon, when they reached a rambling house that had once been an old inn, just as Penny's house had once been the home place on Round Tree Farm. She wanted to take him on home with her but was afraid to suggest it. She did suggest cordially, however, "You must come over sometime, Ron. After we move, you can cut across Gladstone's pasture land."

"Oh, I've already been over to your new house," Ron said, as he divided the books with Marny and got out. "I walked over one day, but none of you were there. It's going to be a nice house, Mrs. Jordon."

"Marny and I think so. We had hoped to move in by Thanksgiving; now we aren't too sure that we'll make it by Christmas. But you don't have to wait until then," she reminded.

"I won't." He gave her a nice grin, and added, "Thanks for the ride." Then he looked at Marny to ask, "Will you tell me tomorrow whether you're going to the game, or not?"

"I'll go." Marny made a sudden decision. She knew her Aunt Tippy wanted her to go to the game, and in a way, she wanted to go. And as they drove on past Parri's she said in a small voice, "Aunt Tippy, I've never been to a football game. I won't know how to act."

"Oh, sugar, of course, you will." Tippy pulled over to the side of the road and stopped the car. "Sit up here with me," she said. "I can't talk to you so well back there." And when Marny was settled in beside her, she went on, "You'll scream and whoop and yell with the rest of them. When your team makes a touchdown you'll stand up and shriek, and when the other team makes one you'll slump down and groan."

"I will?"

"Of course." Marny's eyes were wide with interest; and to keep them that way, Tippy foretold, "You'll stay excited, too, while you eat in the restaurant. Everyone will be talking about the game, and you'll come home afterward, just the way you did after your first day of school, all bubbly and enthusiastic."

"Oh, I hope I will." Marny gave a sigh that was both resigned and happy, before she confided, "I think Lou Anne is going to the game with Ron's brother Hal. He asked her to."

"Then why don't you invite Lou Anne out to spend the night?" Tippy suggested impulsively, because that was what she would have done when she was Marny's age. The whole gang would have poured into her house on Governors Island, or into the Jordons', and they would have rolled back the rugs, and danced. Alcie would have been with them then. She gave a silent nostalgic sigh for those days when she and Bobby, Alcie and Peter, had had so much fun together. Marny was sitting in silence, and she hoped she hadn't pushed things too fast.

"It *would* be more convenient," Marny said thoughtfully, at last. "I don't know where Lou Anne lives, exactly, but it's a long way from us and we'd have to take her home. Do you really think I should invite her?"

"I think it's the perfect solution. We can drive her home on Sunday afternoon and the kids will love it."

They rode along planning what Marny would wear to the game, making a momentous decision between a sweater and skirt and a green corduroy dress, and Tippy realized with sudden pleasure that she had a sub-deb daughter.

10

Marny went to the football game. Lou Anne's father drove her out on Saturday morning with her overnight case. She was a pretty honey-colored blonde who wore her hair pulled straight up and tied with a ribbon so that it hung down her back in a fall.

She talked incessantly, which was good, because Marny, overcome by being a hostess, was almost tongue-tied. "This is just lovely," she exclaimed, surveying the kitchen with eyes that were as dark and shiny as ripe olives. Then, while Marny prepared their lunch, she grabbed Tippy Two under her arms and swung her around in wide circles. Tippy Two's whirling feet hit Cassius on the head, and with a surprised yelp he fled under the table. "Oh, you poor little thing!" Lou Anne cried, suddenly releasing the dizzy Tippy Two to crawl under the table and pet him. Cassius wagged his plume, and Switzy, having been roused from a nap, gave sharp, protesting barks.

Marny, mixing mayonnaise with deviled ham for a sandwich spread, dropped her spoon in the mixture to give Petey a spin on the human merry-go-round. She became relaxed and a little silly, but when the car bringing Ron and Hal came, she looked at the strangers on the front seat and stayed shyly close to Lou Anne.

"Get in," Beverly Whitlock said, not waiting for introductions. "Two of you sit in back and one of you come up here with Allison and me."

Marny scrambled in behind Lou Anne in order to sit beside her, but to her dismay she heard Hal say grumpily, "Move over," then climb across her feet to sit in the middle. She didn't have to talk as they drove in town to the football field that was on a vacant lot near the school and had wooden bleachers along two sides. She still clung to Lou Anne, and after they had climbed up to the fourth row where there were six vacant places, she was grateful to find herself next to her, with Ron and Hal flanking them.

But when the teams trotted in and the crowd began to cheer, she stood up and cheered with it. She had a mimeographed copy of the school cheers in her pocket, but she didn't bother to take it out and memorize it. She shouted when the others did, and when she didn't know the words she came in strongly on the "rah, rah, rahs."

"I don't think it's any disgrace to lose by one point," she said to Ron, when the game had ended and they were walking over the stubbled grass to the car. "Just because the other team had a player who could kick the ball over the goalpost three times and ours could only do it twice, doesn't mean that they *played* better than we did. I don't think that extra-point business is fair." She had become a devotee of football in a very short time, and she forgot that Bev and Allison and Hal were strangers. She crowded into a booth with them in the Pizza Parlor without clinging to Lou Anne.

It was almost nine o'clock when Bev stopped the car in her driveway and she got out. "Oh, I've had the most joyful day!" she cried, as an upstairs window opened and Tippy's head appeared in it.

"Marny," Tippy called down, "why don't you ask them all to come in? There are soft drinks in the refrigerator and Tippy Two and I made a batch of fresh cookies. If you want to dance," she suggested, "there's a good band on the stereo now and you can roll back the big center rug." Then her head disappeared and the window closed.

"*Will* you come in?" Marny asked, eager to have them, even though she didn't know how one went about giving an impromptu party.

The car emptied like magic. Instead of Lou Anne coming in alone with her, all of them hurried in. Coats were shed; they found the telephone to call home; the girls found the kitchen while the boys rolled up the rug. At first, Marny worried that the noise might wake Tippy Two and Petey; then she forgot about it. She was learning to dance. It began in the same way that her shouting of the school cheers at the football game had: she could only stumble into a few steps at first, but she had five willing teachers. And by the time the rug was put back and the house was orderly again, she said good night at the door with her feet still tapping.

"Oh, Aunt Tippy, it was wonderful!" she cried the next

morning, running into the kitchen while Lou Anne still slept upstairs. "I learned to dance. Ron says I'm good—or will be after he gives me a few more lessons. Oh, I do thank you for a simply groovy time."

She sounds like Parri, Tippy thought, watching Marny fly about the kitchen, shaking cornflakes into bowls for Tippy Two and Petey, who sat wide-eyed and entertained at the table. Or perhaps like Alcie, who always looked after her little brothers and sisters.

They saw Ron quite often after that. He would show up at the new house that had casement windows and inside walls to make rooms now, and he had only one fault: both he and Lou Anne had contracted telephonitis. Marny hadn't caught it, yet, so her conversations consisted of brief answers. Too brief, Tippy often thought, remembering the hours she had spent on the telephone, and enjoying the one-sided chitchat in a house where evenings were too quiet without Peter.

Marny still liked to come straight home from school and stay there. Nothing mattered so much to her as the security she felt in coming home. "I guess you don't understand about me, Parri," she said one day, when Parri had come over to scold her for not wanting to come to a party she planned to give. "Your crowd is older than I am. All the kids I know, even Ron and Lou Anne, are older—in their ways, I mean. I don't want to catch up too fast. I have lots of time to do it in, Parri."

Parri never had enough time, so she stared at Marny without understanding, and listened to Marny add in explanation, "I enjoy what I have *now*. Later, I can spread out. Don't you see?"

Parri didn't, and she shook her head. She had always enjoyed what she had and looked forward to having more of it. So, still puzzled, she gave up and left.

November days turned cold. Trees went to sleep, brown grass crackled when stepped on, and Peter's letters, which he tried to write every night during a lull in fighting, were delivered four or five at a time after worrisome days of watching for the postman. Tippy Two was learning to say a few words in French, and Petey brought home an endless display of crayoned pictures, all splashed with red, because he liked red.

"I think he's going to be a fireman," Tippy said, one blustery afternoon, turning back from the window where she had been watching him and Tippy Two climb into the car to wait for her. Then, dropping his last flaming contribution on a table, she asked, "Are you sure you don't want to go over to Mums' and Dad's with us?"

Marny shook her head before she said, "I have a lot of studying to do, and I haven't written to Miss Wilcox for two weeks. I'll have to get that in tonight. You go on and I'll put the roast in."

Her days were cut from a pattern. She liked them that way. She could stitch them into a garment that fitted her. "I'm me, Marny," she would sometimes say when she unexpectedly met her reflection in a mirror. "Hello, Marny." And off she would go in her new clothes and her new personality.

It was on a Sunday afternoon when snowflakes were swirling through the air and Marny was home alone that Davy appeared again. She was sitting on the sofa before the fire, reading a required book, when she heard a tap on the French doors in the entryway to the terrace. She didn't know it was Davy when she sprang up to answer the knock.

She could only see a figure in a long raccoon coat that reached almost to his feet and a plaid hunting cap with the earflaps pulled down.

"Hello, there," Davy said, pulling off his cap. "How do you like my rig? The coat used to belong to Grandfather Houghton."

"It's nice and furry," Marny answered, watching him take it off, and reaching out for it. "Let me lay it on a chair."

"Be careful how you handle it," he said, knowing he was flustering her, and enjoying it. "It's very valuable because of its age. We give it loving, tender care."

He waited while she opened the door to a small closet and respectfully hung the coat on a padded hanger before he asked, "Is Aunt Tippy around?"

"No, I'm sorry," Marny came out to say, more regretfully than he knew. "Aunt Penny and Uncle Josh got home last night and she took the children over to see them. I can telephone her to come home," she suggested hopefully.

"Don't bother. If she doesn't show up while I'm here, Mom and I can stop by there when she drives me back to the Point. I had a swell letter from Uncle Peter," he said, as he followed her into the living room, "and I wanted to read it to her."

He wore a tweed jacket and boots and breeches, so Marny assumed he had been riding his horse. She knew he had a horse, and was almost sure that its name was Singing Star. She thought they might talk about the horse while they waited; and perhaps, somehow, she could slip out to the front hall and the telephone. This was worse than the time he had come with John.

"Wasn't it awfully cold riding today?" she began; but he

had picked up the open book she had left on the sofa and was reading its title.

"*The Decline and Fall of the Roman Empire,*" he said. "Isn't this pretty stiff reading?"

"It's slow but I'm enjoying it."

He was standing with his back to her and blocking her path, so she sat down in one of the big chairs and waited until he put the book down, arranged himself comfortably on the sofa, and said, "Oh, you asked me if I was riding, didn't you? Yes, I was, and it was freezing cold. Sing was full of zip and I really gave him a workout. Do you ride?" he asked.

"I wouldn't know how to get up on a horse." Marny studied him thoughtfully. He was just another older member of the family who didn't know much about her as yet, she decided, so she said, "I wouldn't know how to put on ice skates, either, or water skis, and I'm just learning to dance. I don't know how to do any of the things you do. But I'm learning," she added, since the rest of the family knew that. She didn't realize it, but her little chin had lifted proudly on her last sentence, and because she remembered that Parri had told her to smile more often, especially when it was hard to do, she sent him one.

"Good for you," he said, wondering what they could talk about next. This prim kid was spunky, he thought, sitting there with her feet clamped together, her shoulders straight, and her big gray eyes regarding him soberly; and he ran his hand over his short tousled hair while he searched for some subject that might interest them both. How about Aunt Tippy? he considered. His mother had said that Marny adored her. Or Parri? Parri was nearer her age, and Marny probably saw her a lot.

"Parri can't ride worth a cent," he said, making an unfortunate choice. "I've tried to teach her but she's no good at it." He stopped because he saw Marny's whole face tighten. "Did I say something to get your back up?" he asked. "Don't you like Parri?"

"Oh, I like her. I like her a lot. It's just that—well, just that. . . ." Marny took her turn at cutting off a remark, and Davy prompted:

"Just what?"

"Oh, that you're so much older than we are, and Parri thinks you're a perfectionist. She says you're always scolding her because she falls short of your ideals. I thought you were going to make me learn to ride a horse."

Davy threw back his head, and laughed. He laughed so hard that Marny found herself smiling sheepishly with him. "That defeats me," he said, sitting up straight and looking at her. "Is that why you were so goody-goody the first time I met you? Did you think I'm some kind of a saint with a whip?"

"I guess so," Marny replied simply. And it set him laughing again.

"Look, little cousin," he said, "I'm not so much older than you are—only five years—and you're not a bit like Parri. Now, don't protest," he said, as Marny's mouth opened. "Parri is a girl who can get into one picklement after another. She thrives on them, and from all I've heard about you, you don't, so let's destroy her image of me. Let's start over, shall we?"

"How?" Marny asked simply. And he noticed that her feet came apart to let one leg tuck comfortably under her in the chair.

"Well, let's begin with this. I'm not old enough to be an

uncle, so why can't I be your big cousin? A nice, pleasant cousin who likes you the way all your other cousins do?" He expected an answer, but to his surprise Marny only untangled herself from the chair and went over to the window seat, where she picked up a plate of homemade candy.

"Would you like some fudge, Davy?" she asked, coming back to hold out the plate to him. "I made it this afternoon, and I was eating it while I looked out at the snow and did my homework. Making fudge is something else I'm learning to do," she said, as he took three pieces. And with the plate between them, she dropped unselfconsciously down on the sofa beside him.

They emptied the plate, with Davy getting up now and then to put another log on the fire, and more than an hour had passed before he said reluctantly, "I'll have to go if Mom's to get me back to the Point on time."

She brought his fur coat from the closet; and as he slid into it, she clasped her hands together and said in mock fear, "Oh, be *careful* of it." Then she smiled the winsome smile that had charmed the family, and warned, "You must treat it tenderly."

"That I will." He paused at the door with his unbecoming cap in his hand to ask, "Marny, the plebes have big doings during the Christmas holidays, because they aren't allowed to go home on leave. Parri is going to some of the dances, so would you like me to fix up a date for you?"

"No, but thank you for offering to, Davy," Marny answered, giving a visible shudder that he would be sure to see. "You know how I feel about so many things now that I'm sure you'll understand why I can't go any faster than I'm going. The high school crowd is all I can manage."

"Atta girl. Well, I'll see you at the traditional family Thanksgiving dinner." He went out into the blowing snow, and as he tramped along the almost obliterated driveway to Gladstone, he thought, She *is* a nice kid. She's sweet. She's got a charm she doesn't know she has, and she's entertaining. Aunt Tippy is lucky to have found her.

Marny, left alone, settled down contentedly again to read her book. And when three snowy figures blew in from the terrace, she looked up to say, "Aunt Tippy, Davy was here again."

"I know he was," Tippy said, pulling Petey out of his snowsuit. "We saw him for a minute at Penny's. Did you enjoy him?"

"A lot more than I did the first time." Marny laughed and held out the empty plate, as she said, "He ate all the fudge."

The Thanksgiving dinner was, as usual, at Gladstone. Marny spent most of her afternoon with a restless Parri who wanted to leave and have a date with Mose. Davy said, "Hello, little cousin," then devoted himself to Bitsy, who had come out for the holiday and was going to the Army and Navy game in Philadelphia with him on Saturday. She was spared Lang's teasing because he and some friends had taken off for Florida. It was another delightful first for her: a holiday celebrated within a family circle, and she couldn't understand why Parri fumed and fussed.

The whole weekend went by in a twinkle. Ron gave a coasting party on a baby hill behind his house; and whizzing over creamy white snow was such a novelty to her that when her hands and feet, and even her nose, were stiff with cold, she didn't want to go home. Lou Anne spent that night at Gladstone Gates again, and on Saturday they made a sloppy, melting snow man with Tippy Two and Petey helping.

"Marny, come here a minute," Tippy called from the dining room a few days later, standing at the table where large, thick books of wallpaper samples were spread open before her. "Which one was it that you liked for your room?" she asked, as Marny came in, eating the last of a doughnut.

"The blue-and-white flowered one, if it isn't too expensive," Marny answered, going around the table to turn the pages of a book. "I'd like my room to be blue and white like the guest room you had in Atlanta. I can use the same blue spreads and can shorten the draperies to fit the casement windows:

"All—*right*." Tippy wrote down the number of the paper, and said, scanning her list, "I gave Petey the one with lots of red in it—that ought to please him—and Tippy Two wants pink. I chose the creamy background with the pale pattern of gold leaves in it for Peter and me. I think he'll like it, and I can use green or gold or rose, or any color I want with it. I sent him some swatches," she said, chuckling, "and I'm eager to hear which color he'll choose." Then she said, serious again, "Mums and Dad, bless their hearts, want to paper the whole house for us. I told them they can do the living room and entrance hall, and *that is it*. Trudy insists on buying the stepladder stool for the kitchen and some new kind of cooking pans she has and says are wonderful. That fixes us up in fine style."

Marny looked down at the wallpaper she had selected,

thinking what a generous family this was. Each member had contributed something: David and Carrol the carpeting, Penny and Josh the check for reupholstering and buying new furniture, Bobby and Susan the reduced price of the car, Colonel and Mrs. Parrish the wallpaper, and even Trudy, the kitchen accessories. "Aunt Tippy," she said, "do you remember the green velvet chair you saw and wished you could afford to buy for your and Uncle Major's room? Could I buy it for you, please?"

"Of course, sugar," Tippy answered absently, still critically studying the gold in her wallpaper. Then she looked up. "Why, Marny, you darling!" she cried. "Of course you may buy it. Thank you, sweet. I understand what's going through your mind, and I accept your gift with pleasure. Now, let's recopy all these numbers and give the list to Mr. Steinerson so he can order the paper and have it ready. I do hope we can get moved before Christmas."

They didn't. The furnace was in and faithfully performing its duty, but the carpeting wasn't laid and the wallpaper was still in its rolls. White woodwork was only half painted, and the new electric range, with its wall oven, stood in the middle of the kitchen floor.

"Oh, well, I'm just as glad," Tippy said to Penny one afternoon when they were sitting on two folding chairs in the empty living room, trying to talk above a great clanking and pounding that was going on above them. "Peter wouldn't be able to picture us having Christmas in this house, and he can in the other one. He'll know just where we're going to put the tree and how we'll all look sitting around it. Oh, dear," she said sadly, "we sent his pitiful boxes so long ago that I almost forget what we put in them. Next year, by cracky, we'll all be together somewhere." She got up as a workman called her, but stopped in the archway to say, "Wouldn't it be ghastly if I had stayed down in Atlanta? That Peter of mine is one smart fellow."

Christmas had come and gone, bringing more gifts than Marny had dreamed stores could sell. The ones she gave to most of the family were simple and homemade: full flowered aprons that she had stitched on the sewing machine Ellin had left; ski socks that she had knitted while she studied; decorated leather or plastic covers for telephone directories; and for the children, toys she had bought in the dime store and turned into amusing little bookends for their bedrooms. And early in January, Ellin returned.

Tippy had seen Petey off in his bus, had waved good-by to Marny and Tippy Two when Sylvester and Carli came for them, and was giving the vacuum cleaner a quick trip around the living room, when she saw a yellow taxicab stop at the side door, and Ellin get out.

"Heavens to Betsy, where did you come from?" she cried, flinging open the door and letting in a great gust of cold air.

"From Florida by plane and by taxi," Ellin returned, coming up the icy steps. And before she kissed Tippy, she said to her driver, "Thank ye, me good man. If ye'll just put me baggage in the hallway I can attind to it from thire."

Tippy watched her count out the price they had agreed upon, then meticulously add three dollar bills to it. "Oh, Ellin, you could have called me and I would have come for you," she scolded, after the door was closed and Ellin was ready to greet her.

" 'Twas too early," Ellin said, looking at Tippy in one of Marny's flowered aprons, then at the vacuum cleaner she had dragged behind her. "I had enough of cleanin' the relatives' houses, so I came home to clean our own. Now, if you'll hilp me get me baggage back to me room, I'll hilp ye with what ye're doin'."

Tippy was thankful that Bitsy had left Ellin's room neat after her last visit and that she and Marny had kept it dusted; but watching Ellin take off her coat and hat, she had to say, "We're happy to have you back, dear Ellin, but Daddy Jordon won't be home as early as he thought. Bitsy is going to meet him in London, and they're going to Jenifer's for a couple of weeks; then he's going to Scotland while Bitsy stays on at Jen's."

"He wrote me that." Ellin hung her coat in the closet and slapped her hat on a shelf as if glad it had a permanant spot at last, and turned back to say, " 'Tis good to be home where I have me own children. Have ye been seein' Vance?"

"Not much," Tippy admitted, shaking her head. "He and Bitsy went down to Jonathan's for Christmas because they were afraid Jon would be lonesome for Alcie, and he never stops in."

"He will now, for me cookin'." There was a padding of small feet in the back hall. Plush and Cassius, coming in through the special entrance cut in the back door, had heard her voice and were racing to her, with Switzy trailing behind. "Ah, me darlin's," Ellin said, stooping to gather them into her arms. "Have ye been sad while yere Ellin was gone?"

"They've been as happy as clams," Tippy assured her, then thought it wise to add, "but they missed you." And she had to say, even though she knew she hadn't enough room in the new house, "Ellin, you can't stay here alone until Daddy Jordon comes back. Will you come live with us when we move?"

" 'Tis sweet of ye, child, but no. I have me boys to keep me company, and I'm quite used to bein' alone whin the Gineral goes off somewhire. Howiver," she said, standing up, "I'll be happy to accipt yere invitation to move in with yere children for the two weeks while ye'll be away."

"Ellin!" Tippy sat down in Ellin's platform rócker with a thud. "Did Peter suggest that to you?" she asked. "Did he know that I'm nervous about farming out the kids and suggest that you come back and take over?"

"He didn't need to." Ellin's eyes were bright behind her steel-rimmed glasses and she stood up to smooth Tippy's cheek. "I would have come in time for ye to go," she said. "I'm sure Peter knew that. He's always been a great one for readin' me mind. I came a little early because I was homesick."

"Oh, Ellin, dear, darling Ellin." Tippy jumped up, and, to the accompaniment of joyous barking and plaintive, neglected meows, they hugged each other.

Ellin was the first to break away, and with a twitch of a smile she said, "Now, if ye'll give me one of me big aprons, not a bit of fluff like ye're wearin', I'll cook us a second breakfast and till ye what a tirrible visit I've had."

11

Moving day came at last, but it took its own good time
about it. Winter weather had hindered the grading around
the house and down the lane. It had hindered everything.
It had even delayed the delivery of a second kitchen range
when the controls on the first one had refused to go on and
off with automatic timing. So it was the middle of January
before the big furniture van bumped and lumbered its way
to the front door.

Tippy was sure she had everything beautifully planned.
Ellin was to stay at home and keep the children after
school, and Marny was to be excused at noon. Together,
they would bring order out of chaos, and at six o'clock
they would hurry back to Gladstone Gates for a quick

supper and to retrieve the children and Switzy. But she had reckoned without the family.

She arrived at the house at eight o'clock, early enough to make sure that she had laid enough paths of newspapers over the new carpeting for the moving men to walk on, only to see another car parked where she wanted to put hers. Bobby was standing on the front steps.

"I thought you might like some help," he said, coming toward her after she had coaxed her car onto a mound of hard clay. "Susan is taking Ti Me over to Ellin, and then she'll be along."

"Thanks, but I won't need either of you," she answered confidently, fitting her new key into its new lock. "I know exactly where I want every piece of furniture placed, and Marny and I can take our time about unpacking the cartons—the dishes and things."

"Anyway, she's coming," Bobby said, following her into the living room and inspecting two new chairs that had been delivered from a furniture store the day before. "How come you chose that tan wallpaper that looks like burlap?"

"It doesn't look like burlap; it looks like raw silk, and it isn't tan. It's a pale, creamy yellow to blend with the gold carpeting, and I chose it because I like it," Tippy retorted, wishing she knew how to get rid of him. And to give him something to do, she suggested, "You might turn up the thermostat. But don't disturb the newspapers."

They followed each other from room to room. Bobby drank stale coffee from a paper cup that he took from the kitchen dispenser, and at nine o'clock, right on time, the furniture van pulled in. By that time the house had five uninvited people milling about in it. Susan had left Ti Me and her battered Christmas doll with Ellin; David had

166

suggested to Carrol that they stop by to see how things were going, and Penny had postponed her marketing to make a detour.

Tippy tried to keep calm. She stood at the door like a maître d'hôtel seating his patrons, except that she was placing furniture. "The sofa there," she would say, "this chair over here, the carton marked *Kitchen* goes through to the utility room, and the drum of china does too." And each time the men returned with another load, the onlookers scattered. She knew that Carrol and Penny were upstairs, unpacking sheets and getting in the way of the movers who were setting up beds, that Susan and Bobby were cluttering up her kitchen with stacks of dishes that she wasn't yet ready to unpack and put away.

"Well, I guess that's the lot, Mrs. Jordon," the man in charge said, when she had trailed him to the living room that still looked neat because it held only the furniture, placed where she wanted it. "If you'll just sign this receipt, we'll be on our way."

She was about to scrawl her name at the bottom of an inventory list when David appeared to take the paper from her. "Are all your boxes here, Tip?" he asked, looking over the typed pages. " 'Eight wooden boxes of books,' " he read. " 'Sixteen cartons, four footlockers, three trunks—two wardrobe and one steamer—three crated mirrors, and eight drums of china, bric-a-brac and lamps.' "

"Oh, how do I know?" Tippy groaned, sitting down on the sofa that still had festoons of burlap hanging from it. "The way things have been going, I can't tell, and I've never had to count pieces before. Peter always did it."

"Well, let's make a check."

He and the man went off together and she sat there for ten

minutes, listening to the activity going on around her. Then David came back to say, "You're short one locker trunk and a box of blankets. The furniture is all here so the guy is telephoning the warehouse. They'll either have to find your stuff or you don't sign."

"Thank you, David," Tippy said, looking gratefully up at him. "What do I do about it?"

"You wait until we hear something." And off he went again.

She sat looking numbly about the strange yet familiar room. Her house was a mess. Mud-caked feet had strayed from the papers she had so carefully laid down, and she dreaded going out to the kitchen to see what havoc had been wrought there. She welcomed David's return and his comforting words.

"It's okay," he said. "They've found your things and will bring them out tomorrow. You can sign the release then. I'll put it in this table drawer so you'll know where it is. Did you see where I'm putting it?" he asked, as she still sat with her mind somewhere else.

"Yes, I see it." She had heard another car pull in, and was wondering who was coming now. Not her mother and father, she hoped. All this confusion would distress them. They had never moved in such a slapdash fashion. It turned out to be Sylvester, with a picnic lunch from Gladstone.

"You have to eat," Carrol ordered, setting a plate on Tippy's lap and even providing a linen napkin. "Everything is shaping up, so relax and eat."

Tippy found she could. She was hungry. Her breakfast had consisted of orange juice and two cups of coffee, so after tearing into a chicken sandwich, she looked up to say, "Has anyone seen Marny? The lane is a mushy trail by now, and we brought her boots over here last night by mistake."

"She's in the kitchen having her lunch," Carrol answered calmly, as the others streamed in. "Now, stop worrying. Sylvester is going to bring Ellin and the children over after school, and with everything going so well, we're planning to take you back to Gladstone for a quiet dinner."

"I don't want to do that." Tippy had enough stamina left to remonstrate, "We can eat the rest of the sandwiches and I can drink more coffee right here."

"All right," Penny said, taking her plate and pulling her up from the sofa. "But just look around you at this room. I don't think you have the furniture arranged properly at all. Everything looks unrelated. What do you think, Carrol?"

"I don't know how we could tell in all this confusion," Carrol answered, watching Susan stack the empty plates on a tray she had found somewhere and go off to the kitchen with them. "Has anybody seen a vacuum cleaner around?"

"We brought one over last night," Tippy volunteered wanly. "I put it in the utility room, but you'll never find it under all the boxes that are stacked in there."

"There aren't so many boxes now," David said, moving her out of his way so he could gather up the newspapers and wad them into a bundle.

Marny came in with the vacuum cleaner, and Penny let it suck up the mud that had dried in brown splotches on the gold carpeting. All the chairs were taken, so Tippy sat down on the floor.

"What do you want to do to this room?" she asked, looking around helplessly.

"Well, first we're going to move everything about."

Penny, accustomed to stage sets, was planning for effect, whether it would be comfortable or not. "The sofa," she said, "should be along the side wall, not under the back windows where you can't see the woods. David, Bobby, bring it over here—right where I'm standing."

Two willing movers lifted the bulky piece and managed to by-pass Tippy as they put it in the designated place. "If you put tables on each end of it," Tippy said meekly, "somebody is going to run into one when he comes through the door in the dark." So the sofa was transferred to another spot.

Chairs were shoved from here to there and back again; and at intervals the audience would stand in the archway to survey the progress. "It's not right yet," someone always criticized, and the pushing and shoving would begin again.

It was four o'clock by the time the room suited them. Tippy, still sitting cross-legged on the floor but back out of the way by now, clasped her ankles below her tight black slacks, and said succinctly, "I'm sure you don't know it, but you've put the furniture back exactly the way I had it. And I'm also sure you don't realize it," she added, reaching into the pocket of her green blouse for a piece of paper, "but the room suits you now because it's a reproduction of Mums' and Dad's. Here's my diagram to prove it."

"Well, how could we tell?" Penny said defensively, but grinning at their stupidity. "With all the assortment of colors you've got in here, *nobody* could tell. It was the gosh-awful colors that threw us off. Gold carpeting, a bright pink sofa, two flowered chairs with a brown background, one green one, and one—I can't describe what color it is."

"I know that." Tippy scrambled up to hug her embarrassed sister, and say, "Thanks to you, Pen, the room is going to be done in greens and golds and browns, just as soon as the upholsterer can get to work. He couldn't start until the furniture came out of storage. I know," she said to all of them, "that you couldn't see the room as Peter and I saw it because Mums likes blue. She and Dad don't have as many trees around them as we do, so I want to bring in the sunshine, but it's still their room that we copied."

"Well, bless your cotton-pickin' little heart." Bobby, resting from his labor in one of the new chairs, sent her a salute. "It's going to be a dandy room," he said. "And now that we've arranged it to our satisfaction, let's get back to our jobs. We still have another drum to unpack in the kitchen."

Pandemonium had broken loose in the front yard, and Tippy flew to the door in time to block the entrance of three small figures in muddy boots. "Come in through the garage," she screamed, barring their way. "You were told to come in through the garage."

"We couldn't," Tippy Two screamed in return, as Switzy dodged in past Tippy. "It's full of big boxes and trash all the way to the kitchen door."

"That it is," Ellin said, panting as she climbed over a mound of untrampled earth. "It's truly worse than anything I've iver seen before."

Tippy laughed as she pulled off boots that brought shoes with them and let the stocking-footed children inside. She was relieved to see Marny appear from somewhere, and she said, "Take them up to their rooms and keep them busy." But Ti Me wanted her mother. "Oh, she's upstairs some-where," Tippy told Marny. "She said she was going to do the linen closet, so find her, sugar."

"I will." Marny picked up the shoes before she marshaled

her brood ahead of her, and stood on the stairway to say, "Stop worrying, Aunt Tippy, we're making great progress."

"I hope we are."

Tippy thought about the neat house she had expected to have that night; about the cartons she and Marny would unpack one at a time in the days to come, putting their contents in cabinets and closets where they would know how to find them. And while she was standing there, wondering where to go and what to do next, she saw Bobby come out of the living room. He was singing lustily, " 'Heigh-ho, heigh-ho, it's off to work we go,' " and carrying a box of light bulbs that she had bought the day before.

"What are you going to do with those?" she asked him.

"I don't know yet," he answered with a shrug. "David said that lamps are coming out so have some bulbs ready. Carrol and Penny are having fits out in that library you've built on where a porch should be. They say your furniture is gosh-awful."

"It isn't gosh-awful at all. It's the beautiful rattan furniture that Peter and I bought for our first house down in Panama," Tippy declared, pushing past him to see what was happening in the room that was to be a special family sitting room.

"These flowered cushions have spots all over them," Penny said pointing, as Tippy stopped in the doorway. "They're ruined."

"No, they aren't," Tippy returned, accustomed to hearing that. "They'll wash when I get time to do it." She looked at the pieces of furniture that huddled together in the center of the room as if afraid to be separated; and stroking a chair, she said, "We haven't used this since we were in

Panama. Rollo made most of the spots with bones he brought home from the soldiers' mess, and all I have to do is dump the covers in the washing machine. I almost hate to," she said sighing, "because they remind me of Rollo."

"Well, it's funny-looking furniture for a library," Penny commented, shoving a chair off into a corner where it stopped against empty bookshelves. "If you don't have enough money to buy new, Tip. . . ."

"Oh, I do." Tippy interrupted her generosity by saying, "I have plenty left from the check you gave me. It's just that Peter and I love this furniture. It's the first we ever owned, and it has memories for us. I want it in the room where I'm going to live most of the time—and the kids can't hurt it," she added as an afterthought. "Please, let's just leave it where it is for today."

"All right," Penny gave in, "but you're slowing up the wheels of progress."

At five o'clock Sylvester appeared again, bearing tea, this time. Afternoon tea was always served at Gladstone, so, since no one was at home to have it, Perkins had told him to transport the silver tea service, finger sandwiches and little cakes over here. Ellin's serving of it was not exactly formal. Cups were taken from the dishwasher before they were dry; Bobby ate and drank leaning over the sink; the others took what they wanted from a silver tray and went off to finish whatever they had been doing.

Tippy didn't know when Ron appeared. The first sight she had of him was through a window where flames were making a sunset in the east. He and Marny were feeding trash into a homemade incinerator that the workmen had left. She never did see him again.

It was six o'clock when her volunteer work gang put on their coats to leave. "Are you sure, dear, that you won't come home with David and me?" Carrol asked.

"Yes, I'm sure, but thank you, anyway. And thank you all," Tippy said to the group surrounding her. "There was a time, when everything was in such a muddle, that I was sorry you had come. Believe me, I'm not now. I'm *grateful*. Why, we look almost settled!" she exclaimed. "Beds are made, the dishes and pans are washed and put away, even the dresser drawers are lined with fresh paper. It would have taken Marny and me days and days to do this much."

"Then you go to bed and get a good night's sleep," Penny said, patting Tippy's cheek. "You've been up and down those stairs a hundred times today. And, oh, yes," she remembered to say, "John brought over a casserole that Minna baked for you. It's in the oven if you want to warm it up for your dinner, and he took Ellin home to 'tind her boys.'"

They were leaving. Bobby was carrying Ti Me across the mud that was freezing again now, and as she closed the door, she heard Susan call back, "Remember that Bobby and I are right next door and your telephone works if you need it."

She was alone in the hall of her own dear house, hers and Peter's. She and Marny and the children had reached home at last. She could hear voices in the kitchen, and after listening to make sure that none of them belonged to Ron, she went into the living room for a few restful minutes and sank down in one of the chairs that Penny had criticized so disparagingly.

She and Marny heated the casserole, set the dining-room table with silver and place mats they found neatly arranged in the buffet drawers; and when the children were in bed, they transferred the everyday china to a cabinet that would be more convenient for them. Then they tiptoed up the stairs and stood whispering at the door to Tippy's room.

"I'm bushed," Tippy said, "so it's a hot bath for me and bed. Do you have studying to do?"

"Not much," Marny whispered back.

"Then don't stay up too late." She snapped off the hall light and was reaching for the switch inside her room that would light the lamps on her bedside tables, when the telephone rang.

The switch clicked, but no lamps came on because there were no lamps on the tables, so she fumbled her way around the big bed in the dark, stumbled over Switzy's basket, and groped for the telephone. "Hello?" she said, not expecting to hear a woman's voice with a foreign accent answer her.

"Mrs. Jordon?" the operator said. "We have a call for you from Saigon. Hold on, please."

"Peter?" Tippy gasped into buzzing and static as she felt for the bed and sat down. "Peter? Peter?"

"Hello, darling." Now his voice came to her as clearly as if he were in the room with her; and he said, "I'm glad you're moved but I can't talk about that now. I've been waiting four hours to get this call through and there are a lot of guys still waiting behind me. I haven't much time, Tip, so listen carefully to what I'm going to tell you."

"Is something wrong?" she asked anxiously.

"No, but plans here have changed. I can't get my R and R leave unless I take it right away."

"Now? Tonight?" she asked.

"No, darling, a week from today. That will be the twenty-third here, and the twenty-second where you are.

Do you think you can get ready to be in Australia by then?"

"I can be there tomorrow," Tippy answered confidently, not knowing how she would do it but sure she could.

"Okay, then take down the dope I'm going to give you. Do you have pencil and paper?"

"No." Tippy didn't have even a light, but she said, "Wait just a second and I will have." She covered the mouthpiece with her hand while she shouted, "Marny, bring a pencil and paper and turn on the hall light so you can see to write on it. Hurry, it's Uncle Major!" Then she said into the telephone again, "All right, Peter. What is the dope you want to give me?"

"First, it's all set for me to leave here on the twenty-third of January, just after midnight. Now remember, Tip," he said impressively, "that's the twenty-second to you."

"The twenty-second," she repeated, seeing Marny ready in the doorway with her pen held above a notebook. "Your twenty-third is our twenty-second. What next?"

"I want you to be in Sydney one day before I'm due in. Got that?"

"Umhum. Sydney. I'm to be there on the twenty-first. *My* twenty-first."

"Right. I'll only get a week's leave, Tip, not two as we had thought, although there is some hope that it can be stretched to nine days. An Aussie friend of mine who's been discharged and is back home will meet you at the airport and take you to the Hotel Menzies. You'll have to send him a radiogram giving your flight number. Childie," he suggested, "you'd better get David or Bobby to take care of all your arrangements for you."

176

"I'll get David," Tippy replied promptly.

"Okay. Captain Kenyon Anderson will meet you."

"Captain Kenyon Anderson," Tippy relayed, nodding to Marny.

"His business address is two—two—six—one Crown Street."

"Twenty-two sixty-one Crown Street," Tippy repeated for Marny to write down, "and he will take me to a hotel called Menzies."

"That's right, and because I don't know when my plane will get in on the twenty-third, you'll just have to wait there for me. And remember this, Tip, Australia is across the International Date Line, too, so you'll have to do some figuring about when you start."

"I will," Tippy promised. "If I can't get a booking when I want it, I may be there *two* days ahead of you. I won't risk being late, and I'll have David send you a radiogram when I leave here. Oh," she remembered to ask, "do I send it to the place where you're stationed now or to Saigon?"

He thought for a precious ticking second before he said, "Don't try it, darling. I just came in to Saigon to put this call through. I'll be out with the troops and won't get back here until just before my plane takes off. I'll know you have everything under control."

"I will have. Oh, Peter," Tippy had to take time to say, "I'm so excited, and I love you so much."

"I love you, Childie, and we'll be together soon."

The foreign voice cut in with, "Your time is up, Major," and he could only say, "It's summer in Australia. Good-by, darling, I'll see you on your twenty-second," before she was left holding a dead receiver.

She was almost on her way to see Peter! In six days, no, five. . . . She looked up to ask Marny, "How long is it until the twenty-second?"

"Seven days," Marny answered, her head clearer for figures at the moment than Tippy's, but she reminded, "You have to be there on the twenty-first, Aunt Tippy, and I don't know how long it takes to fly to Australia, do you?"

"I haven't the faintest idea. And I don't even know if I can get a through seat on a plane. Perhaps I'll have to sit for ages in San Francisco or somewhere. I'd better call David right away so he can start working on it tonight."

She pulled the telephone off onto her lap, then looked down in the half-light to say, "I wish I hadn't been so fussy when Bobby was ready to hook up lamps in here, even though he did have all the wrong ones. Aren't there some sitting along that wall under the windows?"

"Yep." Marny snatched up a lamp, any lamp, and brought it to the bedside table where Tippy sat. "Wait a minute," she said, looping its cord behind the bed and plugging it in. But no light came on.

"Oh, darn those inefficient electricians," Tippy groaned, trying to see the dial in the gloom.

Marny was running around the bed again. "There," she said, flipping the switch by the door and filling the room with light. "You turned this on, then off again, that's all. Here, let me dial for you," she said, coming back.

She put a slim, sure finger in the hole where Tippy's had been fumbling, and when she heard ringing tones, held out the receiver.

David answered on the third ring. "Oh, David," Tippy cried, "Peter just telephoned me and I have to go to Vietnam—no, I mean Australia—to meet him! I have to be there in six days, maybe five." She looked up at Marny for confirmation, and at Marny's nod, hurried on. "You'll have to get me a plane ticket tonight."

"Now wait a minute, Tip," David said logically. "The first thing is, do you have a passport?"

"Oh, yes. Yes, of course I have. Peter and I took care of that before he left. I have a passport but I have to have a seat on a plane. And I have to get ready to go."

"How did all this come up?" he asked, being as much in the dark as she had been in her bedroom; and although it would waste precious minutes, she told him. "Okay, honey," he said at the end of her excited explanation. "I'll take care of everything first thing in the morning."

"Not *tonight?*" she cried.

"Of course not tonight." Bobby would have whooped with laughter at her impatience, but David said reassuringly, "I'll go in to New York in the morning when the ticket offices are open and get you set up."

"But what if all the seats are taken?" she asked in a frightened voice.

"They won't be. A lot of planes fly to California, and transpacific planes fly out of a number of different cities there. We'll get you to Sydney on time."

"You're sure?" She was relieved by his comforting calm, but she asked, "Do you think we might need someone like Senator Robinson to pull strings, or perhaps the president of Daddy Jordon's company?"

"You'll be aboard a plane," he said positively. "Trust me. Do you want to talk to Carrol now?"

"Oh, I guess so." She had to tell Carrol how inadequate her summer clothes were. Peter had said that it was summer in Australia and her white dress had come back from the cleaner with a spot still on it. Two cottons had zippers that wouldn't work and she had snagged her best pair of shorts.

"Listen, sweet," Carrol said at the end of her tale of woe, "you're not going to Australia to stay a year—just a week. Sydney is a big city and has wonderful stores. Did Peter give you any hint of what you'll be doing while you're there?"

"He wrote once that we'd go to Rose Hill to the races, and to Chequers—that's the fanciest night club—and we'd take tours through the country."

"Well, then, I'll come over tomorrow and we'll sort through your wardrobe."

"You can't find it," Tippy wailed.

"Oh, yes, I can." Carrol laughed and reminded, "You forget that Penny and I put all your clothes away. Your summer dresses are in three zipper bags in the upstairs cedar closet. The new cocktail dress you bought just before Peter left is in *your* closet."

"Where's my summer-weight beige coat?" Tippy demanded, "and my blue fox stole that Peter gave me for my birthday?"

"I know, and I'll find them tomorow. Just stop thinking and go to sleep."

"All right."

Tippy was doubtful that she could because all her nerve ends were tingling like electric wires. "I guess I'll make it," she said to Marny, "with David and Carrol taking charge." Then she asked, "What will we do about the upholsterer who's to pick up the furniture next week?"

"I'll see that he gets it," Marny told her confidently. "If I'm at school, Ellin will be here to give it to him."

"Oh, my goodness, *Ellin!*" Tippy ran her hands distractedly through her hair. "She'll work herself to death doing all the things I've left undone, and Switzy has a date for a haircut on Saturday."

"Parri and I can take him," Marny said, starting a list so Tippy would calm down.

"Oh, be sure to telephone the grading company not to begin grading until I come back, and notify the Coronet Laundry that you'll leave the bag in the garage, and you'll have to fill in the amounts on the checks I'm going to sign for the telephone and electric lights, and—oh, dear."

The telephone rang, and snatching it up she said, "Hello," in such a quavering voice that it made Penny laugh. "Hello, again, Tip," Penny said. "We've just heard the good news. Carrol says you're in a flap about your summer clothes. But you don't need to be. Cruise clothes are in and I'm going to take you in town and buy you an outfit the likes of which Peter has never seen."

"But I haven't *time*," Tippy moaned; and Penny countered with:

"Of course you have. Tomorrow afternoon should do it. Be ready at one o'clock." And as if certain that someone else wanted the line, she hung up.

It was Tippy's mother on the next ring. "The grapevine is really working tonight," she said. "I'm so happy for you, darling, and I'll be over tomorrow afternoon to stay with the children while Penny takes you in to New York. Susan wants to do it, but I think it would be nice if she could go with you girls. Dad and I will bring Ti Me with us, and you tell Marny we'll be there so she won't have to hurry home from school. Coax Susan to go when she calls."

It was twelve o'clock before Tippy and Marny completed

a list of all the important things that needed to be done, and Tippy had settled for a quick shower instead of her longed-for soak in the tub.

"You go to sleep, Aunt Tippy," Marny said, adjusting Tippy's electric blanket and bending over to kiss her good night. "Everything is going to work out just fine. It always does for us Jordons." Then she turned out the light and slipped back to her own beautiful room that she hadn't had time, as yet, to enjoy.

12

Switzy lay on the living-room floor, flat as the carpet and with his face hidden in his paws. He was such a pitiful object of dejection, that Marny sat down beside him. "I know you saw Aunt Tippy's big suitcase on her bed," she said, stroking his poor tousled head that did indeed need a trim. "And you can't hear us explain to you that she's only going to be gone for a very short time, and that you'll be sleeping in my room and I'll take you with me wherever I go—except that I won't be going anywhere much," she added, doubling over to put her comforting cheek against his. "We want her to go away happy, Switzy. Tippy Two and Petey understand about that, so can't you?"

Switzy said he couldn't. He said it by giving one of the

vast sighs that had been shaking him at intervals ever since early morning when he had seen the gray luggage brought out. With Rollo gone, he never knew what was to befall him until Tippy knelt down to cup her hands around his ears, to look into his eyes and nod and smile, and say very carefully, "You're going, Switzy. You—are—going—with—me." She hadn't done that this time, not all day, even though he had followed her about, hoping for her to do it. She had only run upstairs and down, faster than his arthritic legs could take him. And whenever he had planted himself in her path she had side-stepped him and gone on.

"Look, baby," Marny said, giving him a kiss that he ignored, "Aunt Tippy needs me. She'll never get off in the morning if I don't go up to help her. Do you want to come?"

Switzy flattened out even flatter as if to say, "What's the use? I'm beneath her notice," so she stood up and hoisted him into her arms. "You're heavier than you look," she said as she carried him up the stairway, still stroking his poor drooping head. And in the doorway to Tippy's room, she stopped to ask, "Could you take time out to make a fuss over Switzy?"

"Oh, is he sick?" Tippy dropped the dress she was folding and hurried across the room.

"No, he's all right," Marny said, transferring the limp body to Tippy's arms. "He ate his supper, but he's so sad and mournful."

"He always is when I go off and leave him," Tippy said, sitting down in the new velvet chair and putting him on his back between the knees of her slacks, where he stayed with his paws flopping over like a couple of bent straws.

"I have to go away but I'll be back," she explained, pushing his face around so he had to look at her. "I always come back." And she looked up to say to Marny, "Perhaps it's better to let him think he's going. It will come as a shock to him when he finds he isn't, but I hate to have him mope all night. You silly dog," she said shaking him and smiling. "Can't you be like Tippy Two and Petey? They're all excited about staying with Marny." She stretched her mouth as wide as it would go in a grin, and nodded her head.

"He's sure now that he's going," she said to Marny, watching him struggle down from her lap and go capering about in his old-age fashion. "I feel mean about it, but I can't stay home with him, and I can't take him, and I can't lie awake all night petting him. He'll adjust as soon as I'm gone. He always has. So tell me, sugar," she said, getting up and resolutely returning to her packing, "what shall I take out of all this mess I've laid out? I've packed all my lingerie and the fancy nightgown and negligee that Carrol brought over today to surprise me with, and now I'm down to the dresses."

"Well, let's see." Marny looked over the collection spread out on the bed. She knew exactly which dresses Tippy should take, and was sure this flustered aunt of hers would know, too, when she settled down enough to look at the list they had made together. "The green sparkly dress," she said, "that Aunt Penny chose for you to wear to Chequers, the night club, and the satin slippers to match it. The two new linens and your three old ones that are almost new. You have to take enough for nine or ten days, even though you may not be there that long, and you don't want to do laundry."

"Mercy, no."

"And you'd better have a couple of dresses with sleeves, in case it's cooler than you expect it to be, and a couple of drip-dries that don't wrinkle, for sight-seeing in the country."

"Oh, I wish you were going, Marny." Tippy laid down the dress she was holding. "It would be such fun to show you a foreign country."

"But not this time," Marny said, smiling. "This is to be your and Uncle Major's second honeymoon. And anyway, I'll know everything you're wearing. I'll say to myself, 'Aunt Tippy has on the pink dress when she goes out to dinner with Uncle Major. Now she's putting on the blue one to go to the races, and I think she's going shopping today to buy the fuzzy little koala bears that Tippy Two and Petey want her to bring them, so she'll probably put on the navy blue and white dress.' "

"What will I wear when I go out to buy whatever I'm going to buy for you?" Tippy asked, playing the game with her.

"Oh, the same one," Marny answered, "because you won't want to waste more than one day shopping. You can't let Uncle Major spend his short vacation going in and out of stores."

Tippy was in the closet hunting for a box that held her white jeweled evening sweater when Marny heard Petey call plaintively from his room, "Mums, my throat hurts," and she went dashing along the hall. "Sh-hh," she said, closing his door behind her. And she asked, "Oh, Petey, it doesn't really hurt, does it?"

"I don't think so. I think it's just thirsty."

"I hope that's all." Marny felt his forehead; it was cool.

"Oh, please, God, don't let him get sick tonight," she prayed, pouring him a glass of water from the small carafe on his night stand. "I don't know what I'll do if he says his throat hurts in the morning. Aunt Tippy won't go, and—oh, dear, what would happen then? Petey," she said, sitting down on the side of his bed, "does your throat really hurt or are you just unhappy about your mother going away?"

"It's that, I guess," Petey admitted reluctantly. "I was asleep, and then I woke up and thought about it, and I felt sort of—lonesome."

"You don't need to be, darling." Marny took him in her arms and rocked him back and forth, as she said, "I'm going to be here, and I'll read you a story every night, and we'll play games—tiddledywinks, because you're so good at popping the little disk into the cup, and can beat Tippy Two and me all to pieces—and we'll take Switzy and Cassius over to see Ti Me."

"She's just a baby," he protested. "She doesn't go to kindergarten."

"Well, we'll play school with her and you can teach her to color. And if it snows, we'll make another snow man. You couldn't play in the snow with us if you had a sore throat," she reminded, putting him back on his pillow.

"Then I won't have one. I guess I'll go to sleep now," he said, rolling over on his stomach. "I'm kind of tired, so you can start reading me stories tomorrow."

"All right. I'll leave the hall light on."

She slipped out, thinking, first Switzy, now Petey. I hope Tippy Two won't make a third; and she stopped to listen at Tippy Two's door to make sure that all was quiet beyond it.

"Where did you go?" Tippy asked, when she came back.

"Oh, Petey called for his usual extra drink of water," she answered, "and I gave it to him. He's sound asleep now, so let's get on with our work."

She had never seen her Aunt Tippy so befuddled. She had been that way for four days. She had made decisions, then reversed them. Ellin was to be crowded in somewhere tonight, then left at home until Sylvester could bring her and Cassius and Plush tomorrow. The chairs and sofa were to be sent out, no, left until she came home. The graders were not to come, yes, it would be better if they did. Marny had kept track of the changes, and had rescued pans that Tippy put on the stove, then forgot.

They had finished the packing when the doorbell rang. "Oh, I hope it isn't some of the family," Tippy groaned distractedly. "David said he'd come for me in the morning at seven o'clock, but perhaps he forgot to give me my tickets."

"They're in your brown purse," Marny told her, pointing, "right there on the dresser. Your brown pumps and your brown gloves are there, too. I'll go down and see who's here, and you can be taking your bath while I'm gone."

She ran down the steps, wishing that whoever had come with last-minute messages and instructions had stayed at home. "Have patience, I'm coming," she said under her breath, when she reached the bottom step and the bell chimed again, "but please don't stay long."

She unlocked the door and flung it open; and to her surprise saw Ron standing before her. "I just walked over to bring Mrs. Jordon a Whitman Sampler," he said, holding out the box of candy he carried. "I thought she might like to eat it on the plane."

"Why, thank you, Ron. Aunt Tippy can't come down, but I'll give it to her. Won't you come in?" she had to say.

"Thanks, I'd like to warm up."

The fire had died down for the night, but Marny tossed another log on it. She knew her Aunt Tippy wouldn't need her for another half-hour at least, so she invited cordially, "Here, give me your coat, and sit down."

"This feels good," he said, choosing one of the chairs that had a note and a swatch of cloth pinned to it. "It's pretty snappy tonight. The stars are out, so Mrs. Jordon should have a good day for her takeoff tomorrow."

"I know, and I'm glad," Marny said, nodding with him. "We've all been watching the weather. It's so awful to start off in a snowstorm." She tucked her feet under her in another mismatched chair and smiled at him. Her smile came so naturally now. It flashed out for no reason at all, and she said, "It was thoughtful of you to bring Aunt Tippy the candy, and I know she'll appreciate it. Shall I take it up and show it to her?"

"No, no hurry." He was warm now, and he started in a roundabout way to ask the question that had really brought him there. "Mom just told me that I can throw a blast Saturday night, but before I invite any of the gang, I wanted to find out if you'll come. Will you?"

"Oh, Ron, I'm not going anywhere until Aunt Tippy gets home," Marny said, trying to divert him by being chatty. "She'll only be gone a little over two weeks—counting the time it takes her to get to Australia and back, and the time she wants to spend in Piedmont where a very dear friend of hers lives. Her friend's name is Candy Reed, but she makes her recordings under her maiden name of Candy Kane. Maybe you've heard of her."

"Why, sure I have," Ron said, looking interested. "I like her stuff. She's mod but not too mod. We've got two of her albums at home."

"We have all of them," Marny said proudly. "Would you like me to play one?"

"I don't think so." He was concerned only with the party his mother had said he could give, and he asked again, "Couldn't you fix it so you could come?"

Marny shook her head. "Not while Aunt Tippy is away," she said. And she explained, "This is such an important time to us. We won't see Uncle Major again until late next year, and we want everything to go just right. We want this to be a happy time for him."

He argued with her for as long as she would let him stay, and when he had his coat on again and they were standing at the door, he said wonderingly, "I don't get you, Marny. You talk about the trip and say 'we.' Anybody would think you're going right along with Mrs. Jordon."

"Oh, I am!" Marny exclaimed, leaning against the wall with her hands clasped behind her. And for no reason that he could understand, she asked, "Do you read your Bible much?"

"I did when I went to Sunday school," he replied, bewildered. "I had to read it a lot. But what's with the Bible?"

"When I was little," Marny said, seeing the few happy memories of her childhood, not his puzzled face, "Grandma read it to me every morning and every night. Grandma was a wonderful person, and she made the Bible a fascinating story. Something you said just now made me think that I'm sort of like Ruth in it. Ruth said—in what would be our modern-day language—'I'm going wherever you go, and your family will be my family.' That's the way it is with me, Ron, and even though the circumstances aren't the same at all, I've said those words a lot of times since the Jordons found me. They're my family, and I'll go right along to Australia with Aunt Tippy—and I'll stay right here with Tippy Two and Petey. And with Switzy," she added, looking up at a small black form that stood at the top of the stairway, waiting for her to come back. "Do you understand what I mean?"

"Hun-uh." Ron shook his head as he studied her. "All I know is that I'll have to postpone my bash. But maybe I'll figure you out while I walk home," he said hopefully. "You sure are an interesting girl, Marny." And after nodding his head as if putting an exclamation point at the end of his sentence, he plunged out into the clear, cold night.

Marny watched him go, then closed the door and waved to Switzy, her thoughts already with her dearly loved ones upstairs.